Girl Seeking Beach

A FINDING HOME NOVEL

HANNAH DOVE

PLOTWORKS PUBLISHING

ISBN (electronic): 978-1-960936-67-7

ISBN (print): 978-1-960936-68-4

Contents

Dedication

For those who keep their childhood pail of sand inside their hearts—you know who you are.

Chapter One

AMANDA TAYLOR STEPPED onto the Oak Street Beach.

A hot Saturday in the early summer in Chicago, and the beach was absolutely crammed with humans. There was no smoking, no alcohol, no dogs—these things weren't permitted. But there was also no restriction on the number of people who were allowed on this narrow ribbon of sand.

Holding her beach towel over her shoulder, Amanda minced her way across the field of bodies. There was barely room to walk between the towels. She stumbled once but was caught by a set of hands, then pushed upright once more.

She was looking for her friends. They'd messaged her a pin in a map showing their position on the beach. It was a good thing too, because there were literally a thousand people here. Without their help, it would've been like looking for a single penguin in Antarctica.

There.

Amanda spotted her three girlfriends, sitting cross-legged together on a single blanket. Cristina, who talked a blue streak about every subject imaginable. Tatiana, who had lurid tales of summers spent doing drugs at foam parties in Ibiza. And the grumpy Liz, who was the ballast of the group. She didn't do much more than listen and grumble.

Amanda had known these girls for less than a year. They'd met through overlapping social groups. Their friendship wasn't a deep thing that they'd embarked upon with thoughts of growing old together. It was based on convenience.

"Hey there," said Amanda, approaching the group.

"Oh, she made it," said Cristina. "We didn't think you'd find us! It's so crowded! Have you ever seen it like this? I've seen a lot of beaches and I've never seen one like this. You can't even find a chair at the rental stand because there's so many people—"

Amanda sat down with the three friends. They all wore classic Ray-Ban wayfarer sunglasses except her. On Amanda's face were a pair of cheap tortoise-shell framed sunglasses that she'd picked up years ago at a discount outlet.

"So what are we doing today?" said Cristina. "I vote for drinks at McNichols Rec Room."

"Not that place," mumbled Liz.

"It's great!" said Tatiana. "There's ping-pong and fried chicken and good music and tons of guys—"

"So I guess we're not playing volleyball today," answered Liz.

"Yeah, that's not happening," said Amanda.

"What do you want to do, Amanda?" said Cristina.

Amanda knew the answer right away. "I want to go swimming."

"Why?"

"Because we're at the beach, dummy."

The four girls all turned to look at Lake Michigan, as if they'd just remembered it existed and were seeing it for the first. "It's just so big," said Cristina, "and at the same time it's just so intimidating, because what do you *do* out there, do you just swim, or do you do something else, like what if you don't have a boat—"

"I think it's too cold," said Liz morosely.

"The Mediterranean is so much better," added Tatiana. "It's like, not even comparable."

Amanda grew animated. "Did all you forget what I do?"

"You work for the Environmental Protection Agency," said Liz.

That was correct. Amanda had spent the last three years in an entry position at America's biggest federal agency dedicated to addressing environmental threats. She liked her job, which had mostly consisted of analyzing water samples in search of various pathogens. But she was hoping that she might get promoted to something better, or different—hopefully soon.

"So you care a lot more about the lake more than we do," said Tatiana.

"We should all care about the lakes," said Amanda, taking off her t-shirt. She wore a one-piece swimsuit underneath. It was most practical for swimming and water sports. It also encased her less-than-perfect midsection much better than a bikini ever could. "I'm going to swim while you decide what we're all doing tonight."

She rose to her feet and picked her way through the crowded sand to the water's edge. There, the crowds were almost as thick. Looking north and south, she saw hundreds of people standing up to their knees, hips, and waist.

Amanda waded out past them until she was up to her chest. A young lifeguard in a rowboat nearby blew his whistle. He was looking at her. "Move in, please."

Amanda stood in chest-deep water, facing him. "I'm fine here."

He made a pushing-inward motion with his hand. "You can't go past the lifeboat."

3

"I'm not going past you," she said. "Plus, I was an all-state swimmer."

The lifeguard shook his head. "Move in please."

Amanda felt annoyed. She hadn't been out in Lake Michigan for a while, and she'd forgotten just how strict the city lifeguards could be here.

"Thanks," she said, under her breath as she waded back towards the shore.

At six-thirty that evening, the pink rays of sunset beamed in through the horizontal blinds of Amanda's bedroom window.

She shared a two-bedroom apartment with Robin, a random girl she'd met on a roommate matching site. Robin was never at home, spending nearly every night at her boyfriend's apartment instead. So they hadn't done anything with the living room, which contained a cheap futon and a television balanced on some crates. In the sad kitchen, the refrigerator was empty of everything except condiments and beer bottles.

Amanda knew the apartment could be a lot prettier. But neither of them wanted to commit to improving it, because both knew the situation was temporary. Robin was making furious plans for the future—the ring, the wedding, the house, the baby, the whole pipeline. It was surprising that she hadn't moved out yet. Amanda wondered what was holding up the process.

She laid on her bed, back against a pile of pillows, absorbed in her phone. Their group chat was blowing up. Her friends had decided on a full night of drinking, dancing, and flirting at no less than five different establishments in the city.

And they were meeting in forty-five minutes. If Amanda wanted to join them, she'd have to get going.

She turned off her phone and stared at the purple toenail polish on her feet. Then she looked out the window at the sunset, trying to decide.

The decision came easily. She didn't feel the party in her. Friday night, Saturday night—it didn't matter. She didn't have the money. She didn't have the energy. She didn't have the alcohol tolerance. She didn't really enjoy the dancing. She didn't care much about meeting guys either, not like the others did. The men in Chicago were putting on armor and pretending to be stronger, smarter, jerkier, wealthier than they were. She supposed that guys peacocked and preened because it worked, but she was evidently in the minority of women. She didn't care about those things.

Instead, her mind flew across the city to the beach on the lake.

The beach made her happy. Almost any beach, really.

Amanda picked up her phone and texted the group chat. *Sorry I'm out tonight. Have fun!*

Then she shut off her phone and put the device under her pillow. The girls were going to be upset, but they would have to live with that.

Chapter Two

MONDAY MORNING, Amanda stepped off the El, which is what Chicago calls its metro (short for "elevated") in the downtown loop. She descended from the platform with hundreds of other commuters, most wearing earphones. She didn't understand that. She always wanted all her senses available in the city. You made yourself into a target if you wore earbuds.

She was dressed in a long gray skirt, a light white blouse, and a pair of flats. Amanda never dressed up too much for work. She was a government rat.

Amanda stepped through the doors of the EPA regional office on Jackson Blvd, flashed her name badge to the guard, and stepped into the elevator with seven other people.

On the seventeenth floor, the doors opened, and Amanda edged her way out of the crowded elevator. She entered the large maze of cubicles. No less than fifty people worked on this floor, mostly grunts like her in the open floor plan. Amanda was a GS-6, which was square in the middle of the pay scale, and the people around her were mostly GS-7, GS-8, and GS-9. Around the outside of the desks was a ring of private offices, reserved for the supervisors, mostly GS-11, GS-12, and GS-13. These were the window offices.

Amanda was jealous of those offices for one reason: From their windows were amazing views of Lake Michigan. It shimmered brightly in the summer light and grew dark and moody in the gray winter dusk.

She found her own cubicle and set down her bag. She picked up the sweater from the back of her swivel chair and donned it immediately. The office was air conditioned within an inch of its life. It always somehow grew worse as the day went on, and the building engineers were impossible find. She'd complained in writing once, questioning the thermostat settings, but nobody had ever replied.

Her job was typically split in half. She spent the mornings here, and the afternoons in the lab on the eleventh floor. She didn't care much for either location, because both were indoors, and she was an outdoors girl at heart. But she did appreciate the ability to move around, at least a little.

Amanda sat down and turned on her computer and signed into the secure government portal. Once inside, she clicked on her email and looked at the inbox. There were thirty-three messages that had accumulated over the weekend. Some were administrative, some were requests from private companies, some were follow-ups from people she'd been told to ignore. It was fairly normal.

Then an odd request caught her eye. It was an email from her boss, Stephen Grandulet.

Amanda, hope you had a great weekend. Come to my office at eleven am and let's talk for a bit. I have something important to discuss.

Amanda's heart rate quickened; she forced it slow down. She knew she wasn't being fired. Federal agencies followed protocols about terminations. Plus, nobody was let go on a Monday morning anyways.

She sat back in her chair and chewed on her lip, thinking about what this could be. Whatever it was, this conversation was going to be a surprise.

———

At eleven o'clock on the dot, she rapped her knuckles on her boss' office door.

"Come in," said his voice.

She pushed it open. Stephen Grandulet was sitting behind his desk, deep in concentration on his computer screen. A middle-aged man, he had light brown hair that was slowly going gray at the temples. Photos of his wife and three children were arranged along the bookcase behind him.

Behind the photos was the view of Lake Michigan. Its surface was shining clean and almost heroic beneath the bright blue cloudless sky. She felt her heart leap.

"Hi, Stephen," she said. "You wanted to see me?"

Her boss looked up, startled, as though he'd just been yanked out of an alternate dimension. "Oh my gosh, yes, Amanda, of course. Please sit down and be so kind as to give me a minute."

She lowered herself into the seat opposite his desk and smoothed her skirt. Her palms felt moist and her thoughts were twitching and flittering about. She found it hard to breathe, so she closed her eyes and concentrated on filling her lungs with air.

"Okay," he finally said, "that's done."

Amanda opened her eyes. He was pushing off the computer and had swiveled his chair ninety degrees to face her.

"Yes," she said.

A pensive expression passed over his face. "So, are you enjoying Chicago?"

"I guess."

"Any problems?"

"It's hard to make good relationships here."

He nodded as though he'd been expecting her to say that all along. "Everybody's churning at your age, nobody's settled yet."

"Yeah."

"It's easier when you get older everybody around you has kids. Then people tend to come together for the children's sake."

"That makes sense," she said. Amanda didn't really know where this was headed.

"Do you want to have kids?"

That was a bold question, and it was technically illegal for him to ask. But it wouldn't do any good to object. Stephen tended to overshare about his life anyways, and she was almost a hundred percent sure that he had no retaliatory or wicked agenda behind the question.

"I don't know," she said. "I guess I'm still trying to figure that out."

"You're twenty-seven, right?"

She nodded. He returned the nod but didn't add anything. He should have known that he was in a conversational danger zone.

Then he said, "The best tunes are played on the oldest fiddles, you know."

"Are you calling me old?" she said.

"No, no. It's just something I think about."

She could hear him backpedaling. Amanda fought the urge to roll her eyes. Three years working under Stephen had taught her that he'd been born with the barest resemblance of a filter. Granted, he was harmless, and even supportive, but she had to give him leeway that she didn't to other men.

"Why did you want to see me?" she said.

"I have an assignment that you would be perfect for."

Amanda felt her metaphorical antenna perk up. "What's that?"

"Do you know anything about zebra mussels?"

She nodded. Obviously she knew about zebra mussels: everybody in environmental protection and ecology knew about zebra mussels. They were an invasive species that had originally been native to eastern Europe and western Asia. They'd arrived in North America in 1986 as a stowaway in the ballast water tanks of transoceanic cargo vessels.

They were first discovered in Lake St. Clair, found on the border between Michigan and Ontario. In the nineteen-nineties, the zebra mussels spread quickly throughout the entire Great Lakes region, down the St. Lawrence Seaway, and to the Mississippi River.

"Sure," she said, "they filter out phytoplankton, which lowers oxygen levels in the water. That creates toxicity. Haven't we been battling them for decades?"

"You bet," he said. "What's changed is that we've discovered a new type of zebra mussel."

"It's mutated?"

"Yes, very quickly. This variety looks like it's going to be even more dangerous."

"Oh boy," she said.

"I think you mean *oh girl*," he replied. "We are committed to remaining inclusive in this agency."

Amanda laughed. It wasn't often clear whether Stephen was being funny or being serious. Mostly, he just had an active mind.

"So how does this concern me?"

"We want to send a staffer to investigate this new zebra mussel. It's going to be a fairly long assignment, at least a month, probably two. And we want to do it right away, starting next week." He paused. "Would you like to be that person?"

"I don't know," she said. "Where would I be headed?"

"We've discovered this adapted zebra mussel in an inland lake in Michigan."

"That's my home state," she said, excited. "Which one?"

Stephen reached into his desk and pulled out a paper map of the state. He unfolded it on his desk. Then he pointed to a mid-sized lake in the northern portion of the lower peninsula.

"Lake Batonkin."

Amanda's eyes went wide. Her hands gripped her knees and squeezed them tightly.

Stephen was watching her. "Is there something wrong?"

"It's just—" Her voice trailed off.

"What?"

She drew a deep breath and exhaled. "I grew up on Lake Batonkin, Stephen."

Chapter Three

STEPHEN COCKED his head to the side. "Is that an issue?"

For a moment, Amanda was speechless. How to sum up her feelings about the place where she'd spent all her summers? Her family had owned a small cottage on the lake, like so many people in her state. And her family had been there during all the summer seasons—day after day, week after week, anything you could do on a beach, Amanda did it. Building sandcastles, making driftwood statues, playing frisbee, swimming and sailing and splashing in the water. In fact, she'd rarely showered in the summers, since she'd spent so much time in the water. By the arrival of autumn, her skin was as smooth and as tanned as an otter's.

Then, when she was thirteen, her family stopped going to the lake. There was a reason for that.

A reason that she preferred to forget. That would remain a secret.

When she was in college, her father had died of sudden cardiac arrest. Distraught, Amanda had dropped out of college for a semester. Left without a second income, her mother had decided to sell the summer cottage. They'd fought over that decision, with Amanda claiming that she would find a way to pay the bills on it, but her mother insisted: it had to go. The For Sale sign went up, and within two weeks it had slipped out of Amanda's life, forever.

Just like that, Amanda's idyllic summer life up north was over.

She jerked herself out of her thoughts. "I have a lot of memories there."

"Did something bad happen?"

"No, no," she lied, "nothing bad happened at all. All very good. In fact, they're too good. That's the problem." Her voice lowered to a near-whisper. "I don't know if I want to go back. It would remind me of what I lost."

Stephen sat back in his chair and crossed his arms. "You're our top choice for this assignment."

"That's very flattering—"

"Are you sure you don't want this?"

Amanda wasn't sure at all. "What would I do, exactly?"

"You'd have to gauge the exact nature of the impact of the zebra mussels on the lake, on the wildlife, on the people, on the economy. You'd talk to scientists first. But you'd talk to the locals next, see what they tell you. The successful ecological investigator talks to everyone. And you'd have to write a big report—a first draft, and a final draft."

"And where would I live?"

"At the lake. We'll take care of housing."

She thought about it. "So what do I get out of this?"

"Career advancement," her boss said, without missing a beat. "This is what we call a resumé builder. I'm sure you can see the value in that."

Amanda did see that. It was, in fact, the very thing that she'd been looking for—a way to catapult herself up to the next level of the agency. But it came at a significant emotional cost.

"I don't know if I can do this," she said.

"I think you can," he replied, "and I'll give you until Friday to decide. If I were you, I wouldn't say no."

"Thanks."

He grinned. "You're a smart cookie, Amanda. Don't be a stupid one."

Amanda shifted her weight in the chair, trying to get comfortable.

It was six o'clock in the evening. She'd scurried out of work a tad early and beelined for her favorite reading chair at the Sulzer Regional Library. In this branch was a long second-floor study room lit by natural light from the high windows. It was ringed by reading chairs. This place was one of her favorite retreats.

But try as she might, Amanda couldn't get comfortable here.

In her hands was a book about coastal ecosystems. It was a scientific book written for the average layperson. She was scanning its pages, looking for mentions of zebra mussels.

There was no glossary, so she had to scan the pages. She already knew the basic outline of the threat they posed. But she wanted to know more.

She didn't have any specific reason to read this book—or so she told herself. It was only curiosity.

Amanda wasn't going to accept the offer. That was out of the question. This reading was just to expand her own knowledge. Understanding more about invasive zebra mussels could help her later, on other assignments.

Not this one. Which she wouldn't be accepting.

Her phone buzzed. It was a message from Kevin.

wyd 2nite

Her nose twitched as she read it. *What are you doing tonight.* The truth was, she wasn't doing much of anything, except avoiding thinking about what her boss had proposed. Kevin could be the antidote.

She replied: *nothing wyd.*

The reply came quickly: he was playing kickball. She agreed to meet for a beer after that.

Amanda had options in the city. This was one of them.

***

Just before midnight, Amanda collected her clothes off the floor of the bedroom and beelined into the bathroom.

The sink was clean and the toiletries well-organized. Kevin kept his life in order. It's why she hadn't minded visiting him now and then. If she was going to have a special friend, then she didn't want any drama or difficulty.

He was a decent guy. He would make a decent husband for somebody, someday. He'd probably stick around for his children, the decent thing to do. But he had a problem.

Kevin had mommy issues.

At first, he'd been extra nice to Amanda, making such cloying comments that she didn't really believe him. That was a small red flag. Then, a few weeks earlier, the first snide comment about women had slipped from his mouth. *Of course that's what you would say—you're a woman.* He'd tried to backpedal, and she'd let it drop, but she hadn't forgotten it.

So Amanda had gone sleuthing, chatting with his friends now and then, looking at comments on his social media. She'd pieced together the fact that his mother had abandoned his family when Kevin was in third grade. As far as she knew, he hadn't processed it either. No counseling, no therapy.

She glanced at his sleeping body. It was a male body, much like many others, not too thin, not too heavy. It was a decent body.

Amanda slipped into her bra and sighed. She already was busy reclaiming bodies of water. She wasn't sure that she needed a male reclamation project too.

Her phone buzzed. It was a message from Robin, her roommate. Messaging was the only way they communicated.

Hey just fyi I'm moving in with Chris end of next month no surprise lol

Amanda nodded to herself. This had been a long time coming. Chris was the boyfriend that she'd literally never met but who occupied all of Robin's waking hours.

She replied *ok thx* and put her phone down.

Amanda turned on the faucet and splashed water on her face. Then she put her palms on the counter and stared into her own eyes. She saw a small blemish on her cheek. That needed to be taken care of.

She opened the drawer, looking for a washcloth. Instead, she found three pairs of women's underwear, a small makeup case, and a morning-after pill. Underneath it was a small red card, with the word *Cristina* written on the front sleeve. It was Kevin's unmistakable scrawl.

She didn't need to read it. Amanda closed the drawer quickly. He'd wanted her to discover this, or he didn't care. Either way, this answered the question in her heart.

For a moment, she thought about kissing Kevin goodbye. But the thought of kissing him, or really anybody, left a bad taste in her mouth. On a deep level, it always had.

She slipped out the door of the apartment without waking him up.

Amanda Taylor was returning to Lake Batonkin.

Chapter Four

THE MOVE WAS EASIER than she'd imagined it would be.

First she told Stephen about her decision. He'd nodded as though he'd already known that this was coming. By the end of the day he'd already sent her the contact information about the place where she'd be staying: the Sunset Cottages. They'd booked two months in advance.

Amanda didn't remember this place. That didn't mean much since there were plenty of rentals at Lake Batonkin. But she looked online and couldn't find any mention of it either.

Then she'd talked with her landlord and put in her month's notice for both her and Robin. Technically she could've kept the apartment, found a new roommate, and left regardless. But Amanda thought her life needed some shaking up, and was glad to quit the small two-bedroom. She also could save a couple months' of rent this way.

Then she'd group-messaged her friends that she was giving up her apartment and leaving the city for a couple of months. There'd been a few hours before anybody replied. Then: *omg sweetie we're going to miss you let us know when you're back*

Easy come, easy go.

Amanda was replaceable to them.

She'd found a small storage unit and moved her things in. It only took a couple of hours, since she'd been living so lightly.

On her last morning, she'd left the apartment keys on the counter for the landlord and descended to the street. Her vehicle awaited her—a basic but dependable gray sedan that her father had bought just before he'd died. It'd become Amanda's car for the last few years, even though it was now registered under her mother's name.

As she put her backpack in the backseat—the two suitcases were already stowed in the trunk—Amanda noticed an orange-and-white paper flapping on her windshield. It was a parking ticket. Frowning, she threw it into the car.

This was how Chicago said goodbye.

She slipped into the car and pulled away without looking back.

Amanda maneuvered through the network of freeways. Past the industrial region south of the city, through a sliver of Indiana, and finally into the mitten-shaped peninsula.

The state of Michigan.

Ten million people strong, the northern parts of the state swelled up like a forest of ticks in the summer. The whole state was a summer wonderland, a jewel of the Midwest, with forests, lakes, and beaches dominating life. Tourists came by the thousands for days, weeks, months at a time.

Amanda knew the basics: Michigan bordered four of the five Great Lakes, each one a massive basin of freshwater that stretched hundreds of miles across and up to four hundred meters deep. Altogether, the entire system contained more than twenty percent of all existing freshwater in the world.

But Lake Batonkin wasn't one of the major ones. It was one of many smaller inland lakes that had been scraped out of the terrain by retreating glaciers thousands of years ago. This one was located square in the middle of the northern part of the mitten, in a slight depression flanked by forests and hills.

It was Amanda's childhood lake.

As she rolled off the highway, Amanda rolled her windows down and took in the fresh scent of pine. In an instant, she was pulled back to a simpler time. The memories came back unbidden. Her father. Her mother. Her siblings.

And Elsie.

The intrusive thought entered her mind without permission. Amanda pushed it out the door and focused on the road.

Then she saw the familiar sign: *Uncle Mark's Country Fresh Produce*. The market at the side of the road that she'd stopped at with her father, every summer.

She pulled the car over and, for the next few minutes, exchanged one sad memory for a slightly more bearable one.

Just after five o'clock, Amanda passed a road sign.

Welcome to Lake Batonkin. Population: 2417.

The two-lane road she'd been following, US-25, was the main thoroughfare. The town of Lake Batonkin was a long ribbon of buildings on either side of the road. The commercial zone stretched for nearly a mile, and a smaller side road, Fort Street, ran parallel with it. On the other side of Fort Street was the nearly defunct railroad tracks, which were only used by the cargo train from downstate. It rolled through town at exactly eleven-seventeen every Tuesday night.

Amanda found the Sunset Cottages quickly. She pulled

down the short gravel driveway and parked in the visitor's spot. There were five cottages, each one a small concrete block house with screen door. They looked as if they probably dated from the nineteen-forties. A lot of the earliest structures up here were nearing a century old.

She looked around for an office, or a reception. There wasn't one. But her eye caught sight of a note stuffed in the door of cottage number three. She went over and pulled it out and read it.

Amanda, this is ALL YOURS!!!! Key is in lock. Come say hi!!! - Lily

That was the name of the proprietor. Just below the note, a key waited in the lock. Amanda turned the knob. The door popped open.

Inside, the cottage was a relic of beachgoing days past. It was a single large room with mid-century chair and coffee table. It also appeared to be a mid-century bed—the mattress should've been swapped out decades ago. On the other side of the room was a small vintage kitchenette that looked like it'd featured in a 1940s noir detective novel. It was clearly original to the cottage. A sliver of a tiny bathroom peeked through a door in the corner.

"Wow," she said, out loud to nobody.

Amanda set her suitcase down and removed her jacket. She spun around a few times, sniffed the air. It smelled like a musty antique shop. As a child, she'd been in old summer cottages like this, but they seemed normal. Today, this felt like a museum piece.

It hadn't changed. But she had.

She spent the next few minutes unpacking her clothes and stowing them in the small chintzy wartime dresser. The insides of the drawers carried that old scent of old cigarettes and tobacco.

Then she put on her swimsuit, a robin's-egg-blue one-piece. She looked at herself in the cracked mirror that hung on the door to the bathroom. She was nobody's prize, but she wasn't anybody's dealbreaker either. Though Amanda could be critical of her body—like most everybody she knew—she also knew when to put those voices back in the bottle and stow it away.

Amanda didn't define herself by her body, and she wouldn't let other people define her that way either. She was a full person, with a brain, and a heart, and a future.

Now she was going to dive into her past.

Lake Batonkin patiently waited for her to arrive. Its flat surface mirrored the dusk, with only a stray ripple disturbing the tranquility.

Amanda walked on the beach, feeling the cool evening sand between her toes. It was a good feeling. Her feet had missed the squeak of the sand.

She tossed her towel onto an Adirondack chair and walked up to the edge of the lake. Tiny waves lapped at her toenails. A smile crept onto her face and curled up there like a bashful child.

She bent down and picked up a small mussel. It was a simple purplish-brown shell, but this was the reason for her arrival. She felt it in her hands. These small little creatures, not even sentient, were massively destructive. They cost hundreds of millions of dollars in lost shipping.

She tossed the thing backwards, away from the water. Tomorrow she'd start the investigation. Right now was for relaxation.

She slowly entered the lake. The water was still warm from the heat of the day; the thermal layer wouldn't dissipate until much later.

Amanda waded in up to her thighs, then made the decision to dive. It was always better to get in all at once. She closed her eyes, pressed her hands together, and dove in headfirst. The water sluiced cool around her cheeks and shoulders.

She came up with a short gasp, but not because she couldn't breathe. It was from happiness. More than a decade had passed since she'd been in these waters, and it felt like no time at all. She swam out over her head, which took a minute, then turned around. Treading water, she looked back at the shoreline.

Just beyond the beachline, a furze of oaks, maples, willows, and pines edged the perimeter of the lake, punctuated by large lakefront homes and the occasional lawn. Further down, she could make out the public beachfront promenade in downtown Lake Batonkin.

She felt her heart leap in her chest. Something about this place made Amanda feel alive.

She turned and looked the other way. Down the beach in the other direction was a small promontory.

Her heart suddenly plunged back down.

Amanda knew that promontory. She knew what had happened there. And she didn't want to revisit it.

Amanda swam back to shore and got out of the lake and wrapped a towel around her body. Then she sat down in the Adirondack chair and leaned over her knees, her fingers pressed to the bridge of her nose, eyes closed, waiting for the bad feelings to pass.

When they finally did, she rose to her feet and walked back to the cottage.

Chapter Five

AT TEN O'CLOCK THAT NIGHT, Amanda was laying stretched out on her bed, pillows propped under her head. The remains of a takeout sandwich lay in their carton next to her.

Ahead of her was a small television mounted on the dresser. She was watching the Lake Batonkin ten o'clock news.

She was thrilled.

Young people didn't watch any newscasts, not anymore. But up here was different. Lake Batonkin was the center of a very local late-night newscast. Years ago, it had been a tiny program, and it looked like nothing had changed.

Onscreen, the tinny action news music started, and the camera swept down from the sky onto the surface of the lake. Then it dissolved into a montage of water sports, fire pits, and happy families.

Finally the image cut to the news anchors. Sitting behind a cheap desk were two people: a middle-aged woman with black hair teased up into an odd monstrosity and. a young guy wearing round spectacles with a frightened look on his face. His shoulders were too small for his oversized suit.

"He looks like he's nineteen years old," Amanda said.

"Good evening," he said, "I'm Logan Brent, and welcome to the WLBR ten o'clock news."

Next to him, his co-anchor wore a lightly bejeweled purple top that looked like a piece of formalwear from yesteryear. It was a splashy choice for a newscaster.

"And I'm Violet Carruthers," she said. "Tonight's lead story: a new air conditioner was lifted by crane onto the roof of the new Walmart being built in neighboring DuLac County. Wesley Cruff has the story."

The newscast cut to a video of a crane lifting an air conditioning unit, turning it, and lowered it onto a roof.

That was the lead story. Amanda smiled. She loved Lake Batonkin.

A knock at her door startled her. She went over to the window and pulled the gauzy yellowed curtain aside. An older woman stood there in a sleeveless green t-shirt and rolled-up jean shorts and plastic orange sandals. A bottle of whiskey dangled from her fingers and a cigarette from her lips. Her short dark hair was patched with gray. The way she paced and twitched told Amanda that she was a human spark plug.

Cautiously, she opened the door. "Yes?"

"You Amanda?"

"Yes—"

"I'm Lily," the woman said. "I thought you were gonna come see me."

"I don't know where you live," said Amanda, shaking it.

"Oh I didn't tell you?"

"No."

"I'm in number one. You have a nice swim?"

So she'd been watching Amanda the whole time. "It was lovely," Amanda said.

Lily took a swig from the bottle, then pointed inside the

cottage with an index finger. "You find everything to your liking?"

"It's lovely."

"You really like that word."

Amanda fought to keep her eyes from rolling. "Well, I grew up on this lake, so it feels like a homecoming."

"I hear you're with the feds?"

"Yeah, I guess. The EPA."

"So what are you doing here?"

"I've been assigned to investigate the new breed of zebra mussels."

Lily's eyes grew wild. "Hey I gotta show you something."

She barged into the cottage, past Amanda, and went into the bathroom. She pointed to the U-shape of the pipe under the sink. "See here, this is a bit rickety and it could blow if you aren't careful."

"What should I do?"

"Don't put anything in it. Except water. That's okay for now."

Lily left the bathroom and collapsed in the only chair in the room. She put her feet up on the bed. Her eyes landed on the television newscast. "Sit down, make yourself comfortable! Mi casa, su casa."

Amanda was taken aback. Lily was treating this like it was her house. Which it was, sort of.

She elected to say nothing. Amanda sat down cross-legged on her bed and they watched the local broadcast together. The young male news anchor was recounting the excitement of that afternoon's high school baseball game, accompanied by shaky footage of the highlights.

"Ain't that something," Lily said. "They've only lost once this season."

"How old is this reporter?" said Amanda.

"He's one a them college kids. They pick up that minimum wage and then always move on to a bigger market."

Amanda nodded. That made sense.

"You take ice?" Lily said suddenly.

"In what?"

The woman lifted the bottle. "Jungle juice."

"I don't want any."

Lily reached backwards over her head and felt around in the cupboard of the kitchenette. She produced a green glass tumbler from the nineteen-seventies, the type with twenty different facets cut on it.

"Well good, 'cause I don't have any ice for ya. It'll have to be neat."

Without asking, she filled half the glass with whiskey and shoved it towards Amanda. "You're gonna need a belt of this to get through the weather lady."

Amanda accepted the drink. "Tell me more."

"I don't have to. Just watch."

The newscast cut to the weather segment. Violet was now standing up, wearing an emerald-green cocktail dress. She'd changed during the commercial break, and the new outfit was too small for her. Behind her was a dramatic map of the state. Tomorrow's high temperatures had been stuck to the board with Velcro.

"Greetings, once again, I'm Violet Carruthers, and this is tonight's weather forecast." She stuck out a dramatic palm, punched her hips with it, then pivoted ninety degrees, revealing part of her backside.

Amanda covered her mouth, trying not to laugh. Violet was trying very hard to project a certain youthful image. But it came off as comedic, and it wasn't clear whether she was in on the joke or not.

"Is she for real?" she said.

In response, a hacking cough seized Lily for a moment. It was a smoker's cough.

When she'd finished, she said, "Violet always wanted to be on the television. Her husband's the biggest doctor in town, so he pulled some strings and purchased the broadcast entirely. So now she's our sexy weather girl."

The hacking cough started again. Onscreen, Violet Carruthers was nearly caressing the outline of the state with her fingertips.

"Nobody's talked to her about this?"

"To be honest, I don't think anybody cares that much," said Lily.

The cottage caretaker threw back another belt of liquor. Slowly her eyes squinted shut, and before long her head tipped back in the chair. A long snore issued from her lips.

"Welcome back to Lake Batonkin," Amanda said to herself, and shut off the lamp.

Chapter Six

SATURDAY MORNING, and Amanda strolled through downtown Lake Batonkin, taking in the sights. Over a decade gone, and some things were bound to change. The outrigger shop was new. She admired the kayaks and canoes proudly displayed on the sidewalk in the early sunlight.

Next door, Antonia's Pizza had gone out of business. Antonia had been a tired old woman back when Amanda was a child, and now the space was locked up, the windows were dusty, and the furniture was pushed into one end of the space. Amanda hoped Antonia was still alive.

A bit further down, the used bookstore was still there, Stella's Books, with all the titles marked down to three or four dollars. Romance had been the biggest section whenever Amanda had gone inside looking for young adult. Up here, there was a decided shortage of fit, bare-chested, long-haired men casting about for a woman to swoon.

Next was a McDonalds, which she moved past quickly. Amanda had never been inside that establishment, and she vowed that she never would. The world's crappiest food chain was a blight on the old-time authentic feel of the town.

She passed the post office, a sturdy little cottage from the nineteen-twenties that could comfortably fit four people in line. Amanda remembered following her mother inside to send off packages of homemade summer jam.

Past that came the Bird's Nest restaurant, a local place with lake views out the back patio. It had affordable fish specials all week long, usually trout. Sometimes, in the summer, they hosted an all-you-can-eat Friday fish fry. According to the sign, the elderly were encouraged to attend bingo nights on Tuesdays.

Then she passed the IGA, which was one of the oldest grocery chains in the United States. The company had shrunk to a fraction of what it used to be, but this outlet was still hanging on by its fingers. The store had been in this location since Amanda's great-grandfather had helped open it after World War II.

Finally, she reached the center of downtown and stepped onto the public beach. A wooden boardwalk stretched along the strand for a quarter mile. More than one person had called it the spine of Lake Batonkin.

Amanda popped her shoes off and strolled along, feeling the weathered wood on the skin of the bottom of her feet. The sun was heating up the town, and she held a hand over her eyes while she looked at the sparkling blue lake and clean white sand.

Lake Batonkin, her old friend. She felt something catch in her throat.

For ten minutes, Amanda walked the whole length of the strand. New playscapes had been constructed at intervals alongside the boardwalk. Elderly people rested on benches, wrinkled hands atop canes. Near the water, children shrieked excitedly, running with goopy handfuls of wet mud back to the day's sandcastle construction.

She was at the beach.

At the end of the boardwalk, Amanda returned to Main Street. She passed Camila's Mini Golf, a small putt-putt course that was nearly a century old and that had found its way onto the National Register of Historic Places. She smiled at the memories of going there with her parents. And her friends.

At the corner, waiting for the light to change, she could see Calvary Cemetery, the town burial ground, just on the other side of the railroad tracks.

Another sudden catch in her throat. This time, it wasn't a good one. She turned away and hurriedly crossed the street.

Hill's Drug Store was waiting for her on the next block, and it was like running into an old friend who'd never left town. In an era of chain pharmacies, Hill's had persisted. It was a one-stop shop, from medicines to beachwear to bottles of wine to package pickups. It was a place to chat, to gossip, and to be seen.

Amanda entered the store.

It'd been spruced up. The battered checkerboard tile floor, an original installation, had been replaced with new simple linoleum. A dropped ceiling overhead gave a less cavernous, more cozy feeling to the room.

These changes were good.

She went over to the beverage refrigerator and selected a lemon-lime soda. It seemed like the right thing to get here. Part of her was still seven years old.

Other tourists were already in the drug store, lined up at the register. An older woman was ringing them up. She had short hair and heart-shaped lips. She wore a simple brown blouse and took time chatting with every customer. Nobody was in a rush.

Amanda cocked her head, staring at the woman. She looked familiar.

She waited patiently while the woman checked out the people in front of her, sending each one along with a black plastic bag and a kind word or two.

At last Amanda stepped up to the front. "Good afternoon," the woman said.

"Hi," said Amanda.

Something about Amanda's voice caught the woman's ear. She lifted her face to look at her newest customer. Her eyes caught sight of Amanda's face. She looked taken aback.

"Why hello," she said.

Amanda froze. Was she supposed to know this woman? Had they been acquainted?

"Do I know you?" Amanda asked.

She lifted a finger. "Give me a second."

Quickly the woman scurried off through a door into a staff room. It closed behind her. Amanda was left holding her soda, wondering what she could've done wrong.

Half a minute later, she heard a man's voice through the door. "I'll go out—you let me know when you're feeling better, okay—"

The door opened, and a young man about Amanda's age emerged. He was tall and beefy and moved with a weird grace. Despite the summer heat, he wore a flannel shirt with a pair of jeans. His hair was cut short, and a goatee was parked squarely in the middle of his face. His eyes were gray and kind.

He stepped up to the register. "Can I help you?"

She felt her heart skip. He looked a bit too familiar.

The man glanced up at Amanda's face and paused. "Wait a minute—"

"What is it?" she said.

"Is your name Amanda?" he said. "Amanda Taylor?"

"Are you—"

"It's me, Tyler."

The instant before he said the name, she said it first in her head. Then she went dizzy. She took a step backwards from the register. "Tyler Boyd?"

"Yeah, that's me."

"Oh my god," she replied.

A smile broke out on his face. "It's been a long time. At least ten years, right?"

Her eyes felt glassy but she managed to reply. "Fourteen. I'm sorry I didn't recognize you."

"I grew a lot."

"Quite a bit."

"Thanks—I think."

"I mean, we were junior high kids," she said. "It'd be surprising if you hadn't."

The awkwardness hung in the air between them like a mist. "So," he finally said, "what are you doing back here?"

"It's a long story," she replied. Then Amanda felt the old panic rising in her chest. It was an unwelcome friend who shows up on your door one night begging to sleep on your couch. The one you know you should turn away, but you can't.

She knew why she was feeling this way.

"I don't think ... I just ... I can't do this," she said.

Tyler's eyes glanced left and right, as if looking for the best answer somewhere on the walls. "Maybe we could meet up later. Would you like that?"

Wordlessly, Amanda backed away, then beelined for the door and left.

Outside the drug store, her head a jumble of thoughts and heart an equally big mess of feelings, Amanda walked swiftly back towards her car.

Chapter Seven

THE JOHNSON STATE Fish Hatchery sat in a cleared-out patch of woods about ten miles west of Lake Batonkin.

Amanda was on her way there this afternoon to learn about the new species of mussels. Stephen had put her in contact with a staffer named Curt Hooks, who promised to show Amanda everything he knew.

She wheeled the car down the long two-lane drive through the woods. The sunlight dappled through the tree branches overhead and cast shifting shadows on the skin of her thighs. A tinge of that special smell of summer was in the air, in her nose, in her eyes.

The fish hatchery was a warren of buildings and facilities that had been in this location since the nineteen-fifties, though it had been modernized and rebuilt a decade ago. This was Amanda's first visit, and the biologist in her was excited.

Plus it made her forget about Tyler, who was now threatening to live rent-free in her head.

She parked in the lot and went to the front door. Next to the building, behind a chain-link fence was a wide slab of pavement with two long concrete raceways, nearly a hundred meters each. Those were for the fish.

A man with a shock of orange-red hair and an orange-red mustache struggled across the concrete. He was gripping a pair of plastic buckets, one in each hand. His gray t-shirt was spattered with paint and other stains.

"Are you Curt?" said Amanda.

The man set down his farmer's carry and shook out his rangy arms. Sweat had broken out all over his face and his thin calves looked worn out with exertion.

"Amanda?" he responded.

"That's me," she said.

"I'll let you in over here," he said, nodding to a gate in the fence.

Amanda walked along the fence until she reached it. He unlocked it and let her onto the concrete slab.

"How's your Saturday goin?" he said, closing the gate behind her.

"It's a walk down memory lane so far," she said.

"You from this area?"

"I spent all my summers here."

"Lake Batonkin kind of pulls you in and doesn't let you go," he said. "So this is a fish hatchery. You ever been to one of these?"

"I mean, I work at the EPA," she reminded him.

"Sorry," he said. "I'm used to giving tours to schoolkids. You've probably been to lots of these."

Amanda hadn't, but she kept her mouth shut. For the next few minutes, he walked along with her, pointing out the new hatchery and incubation building. He told her about the installation of four large production wells. Then he pointed at the concrete raceways.

"I was just getting ready to feed the trout puppies," he said. "Wanna help?"

Amanda shrugged. "Sure."

He pointed to a bucket, which was filled with small pellets. "It's easy. We just walk down the raceways and sprinkle the food pellets in every few steps. I'll take the one on the left, you take the one on the right."

Amanda lifted the bucket of pellets. It was heavier than it looked. She struggled over to the start of the raceway. A gushing torrent of water came out of a pipe into the water.

They moved down the concrete channel, Amanda carrying the bucket with her right hand and using her left hand to reach in and toss them into the water. The trout swarmed the pellets and consumed them in an instant.

"I think they're following me," she said.

"Trout are smarter than they let on," Curt replied. "So what did you come here to meet with me about?"

"I'm writing a report on the dangers posed by the new species of zebra mussels."

"Yeah, those," he said. "Well, what do you want to know?"

"What are the fishermen telling you?"

That was a purposeful question. People talked a lot, especially in small communities. The older agency investigators had told Amanda to find the people who spend the most time in the environment that you're investigating.

Curt blew air out of his mouth. "They're saying that they haven't seen anything like it. The quaggas were bad, but these are even worse."

"How bad?"

"They're coating propellers and hulls fast, sometimes in less than a week. They're clogging boat intakes as fast as they can be cleaned out. They filter out the algae faster than ever. And the lake is getting clearer almost by the day."

It didn't make sense to an outsider, but to a trained biologist a perfectly clear lake was a sign that something was wrong.

Amanda had noticed that cleanliness while swimming last evening.

They reached the end of the concrete raceway, which terminated at the fence that wrapped around the property. A few steps away lay the dense pine forest.

"I got half left," he said.

"Me too."

"Switch sides for the walk back?"

Amanda nodded, and she crossed over to the other raceway. They slowly strolled back towards the main building, still tossing pellets into the water. The small fish swarmed happily.

"So what else are you hearing?"

"That some fellas west of here found them in their private pond, so they put the usual chemicals into the water—"

"Chlorine, bromine, potassium permanganate," she said.

"You got it. Guess what happened?"

"Everything was annihilated?" Amanda joked.

"Nothing happened. Sure, the growth slowed for a day, but then the mussels just ... carried on."

"So we don't have any defenses," she said.

"I'm not sure that we do."

"Do you know who else I can talk to? Maybe an old fisherman?"

They reached the beginning of the raceway again. They set down their empty buckets. Curt scratched his head. "There's one I can think of. His name's Sal. He could tell you more."

Amanda had her phone out. "What's Sal's last name?"

"Green."

"What's his phone number?"

Curt laughed. "Sal doesn't answer his phone. He's special."

"How can I find him?"

"That's a good question. I've seen him at the duck park in the late afternoon. He likes to walk the trail going around the small island there. He told me once he was under doctor's orders to walk daily."

"What's he look like?"

He shrugged. "Kinda like most guys around here."

Amanda rolled her eyes. That didn't help. "Thank you anyways. Maybe I'll go look for him."

"You're very welcome, Miss Palmer. I hope your supervisor likes your report."

"Me too."

"One more thing," he said. "I wouldn't go telling people here you work for the EPA."

Amanda paused. "Oh yeah?"

"It's better to not mention the federal government. Opinions run strong."

"Thank you again."

She left the hatchery and headed back towards town, thinking about her next move.

Chapter Eight

A PLASTIC SHOPPING bag in her hand, Amanda stood at the door to her small cottage on the beach and kicked off her shoes. Then she entered. The cool air greeted her inside. Thanks to the concrete block construction, it was the kind of place that would always feel cool. It was also the kind of place where mold and mildew would grow on the pillows, if given enough time.

She turned on the old radio that was perched on the top of the dresser. It was the type of radio that was old when she was a child. She clicked the power button, then used her finger to twirl the tuning dial until she found a classic rock channel. The sound of The Eagles' five-part harmonies filled the room, singing about pretty maids all in a row.

Amanda placed the plastic shopping bag onto the tiny countertop in the tiny kitchenette. She'd stopped at the IGA to pick up some local whitefish. She hadn't wanted to ask Curt to give her some at the hatchery: that would've been unprofessional. She'd also bought some butter, vegetables, bread, eggs, orange juice, and a bottle of white wine.

Dang it.

Too late, she remembered that she'd wanted to buy chocolate, marshmallows, and graham crackers. Making S'mores on the beach over a bonfire was one of the best things to do at Lake Batonkin. It was like being strapped onto a time traveling rocket that was traveling straight back into the past.

She found the small frying pan in the single cupboard beneath the sink and placed it on the bigger of the two stove burners. She unwrapped the whitefish—one of the best varieties of fish—and carefully dried it with paper towels before covering it with salt and pepper.

She unscrewed the oil and drizzled it into the pan. Then she carefully turned on the burner before clicking on the ignite switch.

It didn't light.

She tried a second time. Nothing. She found a pack of matches and tried lighting the burner directly. Still nothing.

"What the heck," she said.

Amanda opened the refrigerator to begin putting the groceries inside. Then she noticed something else.

It felt warm. She waved her hand around inside of it to make sure. Yep: it wasn't working.

"You've got to be kidding me," she said.

She checked the socket behind the fridge. It was plugged in. Nothing looked amiss.

Amanda walked outside and down to the first cottage, the one on the beach. That was Lily's place.

She knocked on the door and waited. The sun sparkled on the lake, only a few feet away. The tiny sound of children shrieking reached her ears, their gleeful voices carried across the surface of the water from a distant beach elsewhere on the lake.

Lily came to the door, cigarette in hand. Her hair was disheveled and her makeup was a mess and one of her spaghetti straps had slipped off her shoulder.

"Yeah," she said.

"Did you sleep well last night?"

"I don't remember. Why?"

"You passed out in my chair.

"Did I?"

Amanda nodded. She was patient. "You don't remember?"

"No."

"I had to wake you up and walk you back here."

"Well thanks for the assist!" Lily barked, her voice coming out hard and loud. Her wrinkled face burst into a big happy grin. "What've you been up to?"

"A few things. One, I'm supposed to find someone named Sal Green down at the duck park," she said.

"Oh, him. Yeah, good luck—he's one a those slippery ones. He don't like no one to find him!"

"But you know him?"

"I mean, we used ta catch frogs together back in elementary school."

"Okay," said Amanda. "I also have a couple of problems. My stove and my refrigerator don't work."

Lily cocked her head. "Neither one?"

"Nope."

"Huh. I wonder why."

"I don't know. Do you want to look?"

She scratched her cheek. "That's probably what I should do."

Lily barged out of the cottage and strode over to Amanda's cottage. She had a purposeful walk, quick and light, limbs straight and oddly stiff.

There, she stuck her hand inside Amanda's refrigerator. Then she checked the plug, just like Amanda had.

"I'll be darned," she said.

Then she went to the stove, repeating the steps that Amanda had taken. No flame.

"I'll be a darned puppy dog," she said. "Let's check the canister out back."

She exited the cottage, Amanda on her heels, and circled around it. There were a few feet of sandy space between the cottages' back walls and the pine trees that lined the edge of the property.

"Holy popsicle sticks!" said Lily. She was pointing at an empty space on the ground. Above it, a hose hung limply out of a hole in the back of the house.

"It's gone!"

"What's gone?"

"The propane cylinder! It was right there! That's why you can't light the stove."

Amanda scratched her head. "Who could've stolen it?"

"Anybody, darling," the older woman said. "All sorts of things happen in the winter up here."

Amanda pouted for a minute. Lily looked over her shoulder. "Oh crap! That one's gone too!"

She ran down to the back of her own cottage. "And mine too!"

"Don't you ever cook?"

"Naw," she shouted back, "I just microwave! Man I can't believe this!"

Lily was still shouting to herself as Amanda turned and went back into the cottage.

She put on her shoes and climbed into her car and went out for lunch.

Chapter Nine

TWENTY MINUTES LATER, Amanda was seated at a table at the Bird's Nest. The tables on the patio had been occupied, so she'd taken an inside table. A warm feeling suffused her heart as she looked around.

The décor hadn't changed in sixty years.

It was Great Lakes rustic. Stick furniture. Ceramic fish. Thick nautical ropes pinned to the wooden pine walls, which still smelled of sap, if you got close enough. The older waitresses worked all year round, their thick forearms balancing four dishes at a time. The younger ones were college students recruited as summer help.

And right there, just off the patio, was the squeaky sand beach.

The waitress, one of the young ones, brought over her perch, fries, and side of coleslaw. It was nearly three pm, and Amanda was famished.

"Can I get you anything else?"

"Not right now," said Amanda.

"Enjoy."

Using her knife, Amanda cut up the three small fried fish

and dipped each piece in tartar sauce. She savored each bite. It was crunchy, creamy, fishy deliciousness. She was whisked backwards in time to all the other fried perch that she'd laid onto her tongue in her life. That was the flavor of Lake Batonkin.

The young waitress returned. "Sorry, but can I ask what your name is?"

"Amanda."

She turned and nodded at a couple of the older waitresses who'd gathered near the kitchen door. They were looking at Amanda and conferring in low voices.

"Why?" said Amanda.

"I think they used to know you or something," she said.

Amanda didn't recognize either of them, but now she felt self-conscious. She wasn't sure what to do next.

Then she didn't have to decide, because one of the older waitresses came over. "Hey hon, good to see you again—you don't remember me, but I'm Candace. I knew your daddy. I used to serve him and you and your family at that table right over there."

She pointed at a table near the fireplace.

"Oh really?" said Amanda, midbite.

"I was real sorry when he passed. He was a good man." Candace paused. Then she said, "So how're you? Everything good?"

Amanda waved a fork in the air. "Yeah, I'm doing fine." What else to say to a waitress she didn't remember?

"All right, just wanted to say hi. You enjoy your meal and come back anytime."

She refilled Amanda's water, then moved along. Amanda suddenly remembered what she could ask.

"Candace?" she said.

The older woman turned around. Amanda gestured for her to come back.

"Yeah hon," said Candace.

"There's something else. I'm here doing some research on the new invasive zebra mussels. Do you know anything about them?"

"I don't personally," she said. "But the fishermen sure do."

"Where can I talk to them?"

"Go to Handley's Market. They gather on the patio out back."

Amanda smiled. "Thanks a bunch."

"Anything to help. Your daddy was a real stand-up fella."

Her mouth opened like she wanted to say something else. Finally Candace turned and left.

The way she said it, Amanda was left half wondering just how good her daddy had been to this woman.

Handley's Market was about a mile outside of downtown. It was situated on a gravel road that wound along the banks of the Trebuchet River, which fed into Lake Batonkin.

Amanda didn't remember the market, but she remembered inner tubing on the Trebuchet River. She'd gone twice. The first time, it'd been too hot, and she'd gotten sunburned. The second time, it'd been too cloudy and cold and her bottom had nearly frozen in the river. After that, she'd decided that inner tubing wasn't as much fun as it seemed and declined all further offers.

The market was a glorified shack with an extension built onto the side. It sold smoked fish, fresh fish, lure, tackle, bait, and any accoutrement you needed for a good day with the rod. The building had red weathered siding and a dirty water bowl for dogs. A sleeping spaniel didn't even so much as twitch as Amanda walked past it and entered the store.

Amanda was enveloped in a wave of fish smell. It wasn't

bad, but it wasn't good either. She'd always thought that fish was the only thing on earth that could go either way, depending on the dose.

"Good afternoon!" a voice boomed out.

She turned. Behind her, was a short man with large glasses and a large, bushy beard. He was as slim as a fork and as tall as an eighth grader. The most notable thing were his eyes. They were magnified through the thick glasses, and he was looking at her with force. He was stocking a shelf with visors.

"Hi," she said. "Are you Handley?"

"Harold Handley," he replied. "That's my name—call me late, call me early, but always call me for supper."

"It's a pleasure." She turned away and began looking through the shelves.

"First time here?" he asked. He had a radio announcer's voice.

"Yep."

"Long time listener, first time caller."

"You've got quips for everything, don't you?"

Harold walked up to Amanda, puffed up his chest. He looked up into her face. He was a full two inches shorter.

"Are you going to buy something? Or are you going to force me to continue entertaining you?"

"You can keep your entertainment," she said, "and give me some information instead."

"About what?"

"About the invasive zebra mussels."

Harold narrowed his eyes. Then he grabbed her hand. "Follow me."

Before she could react, Amanda felt herself yanked by the hand across the store and out the back door. Harold led her down a short, paved path to the edge of the river. The water wasn't too wide here, maybe a hundred feet, but it was wide enough for a fixed aluminum dock built out over the water. A few small boats were already tied up.

In the middle of the dock were a group of older men sitting around in white plastic chairs. Their leathery necks and forearms and grizzled hair told her that these men spent a lot of time outdoors, most likely on their boats.

Harold pointed at them. "Those men will tell you everything you ever wanted to know."

Chapter Ten

SHE FOLLOWED Harold up the gangplank onto the aluminum dock. The panels banged softly beneath their feet. The men were enjoying their beers in a group, a blue cooler sitting in the middle of the circle on the floor.

"Fellas," said Harold, "I'm gonna crack open this boys' club for a minute and introduce—"

He looked at Amanda. She could see the realization dawn in his eyes that he hadn't asked her name.

"—Gertrude," he said.

"Nice to meet you, Gertrude," said one man.

Amanda held up her palms. "No, my name isn't Gertrude. Harold just made that up and I don't know why. My name is Amanda and—"

"But Gertrude is how you've been introduced," said another, "so Gertrude it is."

"It's too late to learn another name now—"

"Gertrude's a pretty name—"

"Is it?"

"I think so—"

"I think she looks more like a Kathy—"

"She's too young for a Kathy—"

"No she's not—"

"How many Kathys do you know under the age of sixty—"

"I know *thirty-nine* Kathys under the age of sixty—"

"That's a fisherman's lie, right there boy—"

Someone opened the blue cooler and pulled out a cold bottle of beer from the ice and passed it over to Amanda. She tried to open it with her hands.

"There's a bottle opener over—"

"Shh, don't tell her, let her find it—"

"Where's the bottle opener, where could it be—"

The men enjoyed a game of *warmer-colder* as Amanda moved around the dock looking for the bottle opener. At last she located it, hanging by a string from a hook on a pole. She popped open the beer.

"Success," said one man.

"Have a seat and tell us about yourself, Gertrude," said another.

Amanda came back and accepted a plastic chair. She got a better look at the four old fishermen. "Well, I've been coming up here since I was a little girl."

"That's nice—"

"You and forty thousand other people—"

"Why did you want to meet a group of old fisherman?"

"Because we're so sexy, obviously—"

"And wealthy—"

"The same reasons we draw all the women—"

"Get in line, hun—"

They were having fun with the conversation, and Amanda struggled to control the topic. But something told her that she shouldn't mention her job, at least not yet. So she let the question pass for the moment.

Then one of the men brought it up again. "Seriously, Gertrude, why are you here?"

"I'm supposed to learn about these mussels for my master's thesis," she lied. She was surprised at how easily it came out.

"Master's in what?"

"Biology," she lied again, "with a concentration in aquatic science."

The truth was that Amanda had already earned that degree. She'd graduated with it three years ago.

"Have any of you been to the pier downtown?"

"Why would we go to that federal mess?" one said.

"Built with a gun to the taxpayers' heads."

Amanda shrugged. "People seem to like it."

"People don't know what they like," one said.

"Give 'em a plate of refried cow pucky and they'd eat it up—"

That sealed it. She decided that this group would never know that she worked for the EPA. It wasn't a good idea to announce to a group of old conservative outdoorsmen that you worked for the federal government, their most hated enemy. Even if she was here for a good reason.

"I'm here to learn about the new zebra mussels."

The group went silent. She'd killed the vibe.

"Well, they're a serious problem," one said.

The others nodded solemnly.

"Worse than the old zebra mussels?" she asked.

"The quaggas were worse than the original zebras," said another, "and these are worse than the quaggas."

"They grow fast—"

"These waters are growing so clear, it's like the Caribbean—"

"We get half the catch we did two years ago—"

"Power plant on the other side of the lake had to take out a loan to pay for the extra cleaning on their intakes—"

"Then they laid off seven people—"

She'd gotten them started, and now the fishermen were sharing everything they knew. Amanda pulled out her phone and began typing notes to herself on her notes app.

"Where do they seem to be flourishing?" she asked.

One of the men pointed at the river beneath their feet. "Right here. These waterways are packed with 'em. The lake too, but mostly they start here."

One man, a rotund fellow with a white beard and piercing blue eyes, was staring at Amanda. "This new species has a striped pattern beneath each hinge. You can see right under that first membrane. Do you know what I mean?"

Amanda tried to visualize the shell. "I can't see it."

"Well, if you can scoop some up, I'll show you."

Amanda went over to the edge of the dock and looked down. "They're right here on the river bottom?"

"That's right. It's about four feet."

She was wearing a swimsuit underneath her t-shirt and shorts. It was a good habit at Lake Batonkin, especially for an aquatic creature like Amanda. You never knew when you were going to decide to pop into the water.

"I'm on it," she said.

Amanda lifted her shirt off her body, and the older fishermen went respectfully silent and averted their eyes. Then she stepped out of her shorts and placed them carefully next to her sandals. She turned around and climbed down the short ladder into the water.

The river water was warm, even warmer than the lake water, and Amanda's legs were immediately engulfed by waves of ticklish grasses that grew on the river bottom. As her feet went further down, she felt the shells of the zebra mussels scraping against her ankles.

At the river bottom, she sunk into a thick muck of algae, mud, and crunchy mussel shells.

The fishermen were looking at her. "Well, Gertrude ain't afraid to get dirty."

"She's a good one," another said.

"One minute," said Amanda. She took a deep breath and plunged her body under the water. She scrabbled around with her hands at the bottom of the river, the grasses brushing her face, until she found pockets of the zebra mussels.

She emerged from the water and held both handfuls of mussels up in the air. Her hair was plastered down the sides of her head. The fishermen applauded. She wasn't sure if they were being sarcastic or not.

Amanda reached up and dumped the mussels on the floor of the dock. Then she climbed back up the ladder. One of the men handed her a small towel, but she turned it down.

The rotund fisherman with the piercing blue eyes lifted one of the mussels and cracked it open. Amanda stood before him, peering down at it. His thick thumbs were gently peeling off a membrane.

"See here," he was saying, "under this, right up against the hinge, you'll see the, uh, the..."

His voice trailed off, and he seemed to be at a loss for words. Amanda lifted her eyes to his face. The bearded man's blue eyes were fixed upon her upper left chest.

He wasn't looking at her breast. He was looking at her tattoo. It read *Elsie*. She'd gotten the tattoo the week after her eighteenth birthday.

"Who is Elsie?" he asked.

"It's someone I used to know," Amanda answered. "Why?"

His mouth opened and shut for a moment, like a fish gasping for breath. "That was my daughter's name."

They looked at one another, a sudden realization dawning on both of them.

"Are you," the man said, "*that* Amanda?"

Chapter Eleven

THAT AMANDA.

The bearded man's words had echoed in her head as she drove back to her cottage. The word *that* felt so strange and accusatory.

But she'd played dumb. She'd told him that he was mistaken, that Elsie had been the name of her grandmother. She wasn't sure if the man had believed her, but no matter. She made sure that the visit was soon finished, the beer bottle emptied and recycled, a round of thank-yous voiced.

Then she'd beelined back to her vehicle.

Now, on the road, she turned on the radio. A high-energy pop song from her high school days came on the radio. Amanda cranked it up and began singing along. Her voice was terrible, no pitch whatsoever, but she didn't care.

She needed to forget.

Coming up on the left was a church, St. Martin of the Lake. It was where she used to come with her parents on Sundays, dressed in uncomfortable church clothes and tight shoes. It'd been her father's insistence. He'd been a strict Catholic.

There were cars pulling into the lot. She glanced at the time. It was five pm on Saturday—the hour of power. Many Catholics viewed five pm Saturday as a more convenient time for mass than Sunday morning.

Something was calling to her. An urge to revisit where she came from.

Amanda pulled over and into the simple gravel lot next to the building. She got out of the car and hesitantly walked up the main steps into the church. She felt self-conscious about her clothing: her hair was still damp, and her wet swimsuit clung to her t-shirt.

God would forgive her—for her clothing, at least.

Maybe not for other things.

Inside, the church hadn't changed either. She saw the same two columns of pews, left and right, about thirty rows each, and a long aisle down the middle. The walls were still gray and undecorated, but behind the modest altar was an enormous floor-to-ceiling window, revealing a spectacular view of the Lake Batonkin.

A quick head count told her that about a hundred and fifty of the faithful were in attendance. That number was much lower in the winter. In the summer, the population of the town swelled, which included more devout tourists to make St. Martin of the Lake their summer worship center.

Amanda took a seat in a pew in the second-to-last row. Her knees brushed the hymnals in the pew in front of her. A moment later, a woman began playing a piano up near the altar, and everybody stood up. The priest came down the aisle, flanked by two altar boys—one holding a large red Bible, the other carrying a crucifix the size of a person.

They proceeded to the front. One boy placed the book on the altar, the other placed the crucifix in a stand on the floor.

Amanda knew how this went. She'd been raised in the church, and the parts of the mass were as familiar as the backs of her hands. For the next hour, she sang the songs, kneeled at the right times, listened to the homily, and shook hands with the people around her. She even said a little prayer inside her head.

For Elsie.

Time came for communion, and Amanda joined the double line going down the central aisle to where the priest stood with the little wafers. She shuffled forward, keeping her hands folded, trying to look serious.

She accepted the wafer on her tongue from the priest, took an obligatory sip of wine, and circled around to walk back to her seat.

Then she sucked in her breath.

It was Tyler Boyd. He was sitting right there in the third pew, next to his mother.

He looked up and they locked eyes. His mouth opened a bit in surprise.

Amanda quickened her pace. She didn't return to her seat in the pew. She kept walking, out the front door, and down the steps.

Outside, she broke into a short run to her car. She threw herself into the driver's seat and slammed the door shut. She started up the engine and sat back and covered her face with her hand. Her other hand grabbed a big fistful of her own hair and twisted.

"Amanda," said a voice.

She opened her eyes. Tyler had left the church too. He was

walking towards her across the small parking lot. He was wearing a utility shirt and jeans and boots. His hair was a bit messy and he looked concerned.

"Roll down your window," he said, making a little circular motion with his index finger.

Amanda sighed and rolled down her window. He crouched down next to her car. His face seemed to fill the window. She could see the stubble on his cheeks, nearly count the eyelashes above his blue eyes.

"What," she said.

"I think we need to talk. Don't you?"

Amanda sighed again. She couldn't meet his eyes.

"About what?"

"You know about what."

She bit her lip and cast her eyes far out to the lake. She didn't want to say yes, but she didn't want to say no.

"Meet me tonight at the pier," he said. "Are you busy?"

"No."

"Me neither. How about seven thirty?"

She lifted her palms. "Sure."

"Good. I'll see you then. We'll get ice cream!"

Tyler bounced up to his feet, waved goodbye, and ran back to the church. His mother was already coming down the steps. He went and offered his arm. She took it and navigated down to the ground.

Amanda wiped the tears from her eyes. Then she put the car in drive and pulled out.

Chapter Twelve

IN THE SMALL bathroom at her beach cottage, Amanda couldn't get her arms above her head to brush her hair.

Her body felt fine. It was the narrow and cramped bathroom that was the problem. Between the toilet and the shower, there wasn't enough room to move, not even lift her arms. Even an airplane bathroom was roomier than this.

Her shower had lasted two minutes. She'd barely gotten the shampoo out of her hair when the hot water ran out. She'd known to go quickly—the hot water tank in the corner of the cottage was about the size of a large jug of water—but she thought she'd have more time. From now on, she'd start splitting her showers in two—one in the morning for the body, one in the evening for the hair.

Amanda backed into the main room and combed her hair from there. Towel around her body, she rummaged through her things, looking for her hair dryer. It wasn't to be found.

"Dammit," she said. She must've accidentally put her hair dryer into storage back in Chicago.

Amanda went over to the dresser and pulled out the bottom drawer. She remembered seeing an extra hair dryer there. Sure enough, an ancient, flimsy model awaited her. It looked older than her.

She plugged the hair dryer into the wall and flipped the power switch. It made a *zzt* sound and died in her hands. At the same second, the electricity in the cottage died simultaneously—lights, clock, television, everything.

Amanda spun around. "You have to be kidding me."

It wasn't dark yet—the sun didn't set until past nine pm at this time of the year—but she flipped on her phone's flashlight anyways. She pawed through her clothing until she found a simple but modest yellow sundress. She put it on with a pair of flats. Then she went to the window and applied a touch of makeup in a handheld mirror.

Angling the mirror, Amanda saw the reflection of Lake Batonkin, children playing down the beach. She turned it back towards herself. Her face was older now.

She put her makeup away and grabbed her purse and went outside.

She walked down the sand and knocked on Lily's door again. "Hey Lily?"

"What?" came the irascible voice from inside.

"It's Amanda," she said.

"Who?"

"I'm staying down in three," she said, raising her voice.

"Yeah?"

"Do you want to open the door?"

"No."

Amanda shifted her weight, exasperated. "Listen, I blew a fuse. There's no electricity."

"So what do you want?"

"I want you to fix it."

"Why?"

Amanda clenched her fists. "Because it's your property, Lily. You're the owner. And I'm living here."

"Yeah?"

Amanda gave up. "You know, I'll come back when you're in a better mood."

"Okay, Miranda."

"It's *Amanda*." She paused. "Lily, can I use your blow dryer?"

"Why?"

"Because there's no electricity in my cottage."

"Where?"

The manager was a lost cause. Amanda held her tongue, turned, and left. She'd meet Tyler with wet hair and pray it dried decently.

She hadn't even reached the pier yet when she saw Tyler. He was playing on the beach with two children, one boy and a toddler girl.

Amanda stepped off the wooden boardwalk and crossed the sand. "Hey," she said.

He looked up and saw her. "Hey Amanda," he said. "How're you doing?"

"I'm okay," she said. "Are you these your kids?"

The question took him aback. "No, these are my neighbor's kids. Their mom is over at the concession stand. I'm just helping out for a minute."

"Oh."

"I don't have kids, in case you were wondering. Were you?"

Amanda blinked, lowered her face. "Honestly, I was."

The boy came after Tyler with a plastic sword, yelling, and

Tyler gently flipped him over onto his back in the sand. He giggled. Then the toddler proudly pranced forward wielding a plastic bucket. Tyler took the bucket and stuck it on the girl's head and spun her around once. The kid fell to her knees in the sand.

"Nice," Amanda said.

"You wanna pop a squat?" he said, gesturing to the sand.

"Here?"

"Until their mom gets back," he said.

Tyler unrolled a towel. Amanda sat down cross-legged, sure to keep her dress covering herself. She loved summertime in the higher latitudes. Seven thirty pm, and children were still playing on the beach.

"So what are the plans tonight?" she said.

"We're gonna get a hot dog together," he said, "then play some mini golf. Mostly we'll just avoid talking about you-know-what."

Amanda gave a thumbs up. "Sounds like a winner."

"I know what I'm doing."

"So your family bought Hill's Drugs," she said. "How did that happen?"

Tyler was on his knees in the sand, the two kids climbing onto his back. "You remember old Mrs. Hill? Edna?"

"Yeah."

"She passed away five years ago. Her kids didn't want the store, so they put it up for sale. I thought it would be a good investment. I didn't need to build up the business or anything—"

"It's a local institution—"

"You got that right."

"So—any problems?"

He thought about it. "We take a lot more packages than we used to. Sometimes I feel like we're a pick-up location for that certain company in Seattle." The two children fell from Tyler's back onto the sand, laughing.

Amanda smiled. She found herself warming up to Tyler again, despite everything that had happened. They hadn't seen each other since junior high, and she was surprised to see that he'd developed into a normal, well-adjusted human.

She wasn't prepared for that. That made it harder to sweep him under the rug.

A young woman with a body full of doodle tattoos crossed the sand towards them. Amanda guessed it was their mother. She was carrying two popsicles.

"Who's ready for rocket pops?"

The children shrieked and ran toward her. She handed each a different one. "I know you wanted otter pops but I wasn't gonna buy those at no concession stand because we got them at home."

Her eyes found Amanda and she suddenly grew wary.

"This is Amanda," said Tyler, "she's a childhood friend."

"Rachel," said the woman. "Pleased to meet you."

"Likewise," said Amanda, but she got the sense that Rachel wasn't pleased at all to meet her. She seemed protective of her neighbor Tyler.

"You just stayin' here for the week?"

"Longer than that. I'm not sure when I'm leaving." She looked at Rachel's children. "Your kids are really cute."

"They always look cute when they know they're going to ... McDonalds!"

Her older child wrapped himself around her leg and shouted "McDonalds!" at the top of his voice.

"Calm down and we'll go soon," she said. "Maybe Miss Amanda will meet us there too."

"No, she won't," said Amanda, laughing.

"No? Why not?"

"McDonalds makes me sick. I can't stand it."

"Well, suit yourself," said Rachel.

"We're gonna take off anyways," said Tyler, putting one foot in the sand in a kneeling position, then pulling himself up to his height. "Tell Chance I'll be over tomorrow to pick up the bait and tackle he borrowed."

"I'll ask him to leave it out for ya," said Rachel.

"Even better," he said. "See you."

Tyler crooked his head, and Amanda found herself following him over the sand.

Chapter Thirteen

ANNIE'S HOT DOGS was a local institution. Inside the restaurant, Amanda and Tyler sat opposite one another in a vinyl booth. A telephone waited on its cradle on the wall between them.

"You know what you want?" he said.

"The same thing as when we were kids," she said. "Foot-long with relish and curly fries and root beer."

Tyler picked up the phone. "Yeah, we'll take two foot-longs, one with relish, one with ketchup, two curly fries, and two root beers. Thanks."

He hung up. It was the only eating establishment that Amanda had ever seen where you ordered from a phone at the table.

"Good to see some things don't change," she said.

"They tried to take out the phones a few years ago," he said, "but there was an outcry."

A waitress brought the root beers.

"I would've protested too," said Amanda, taking a quaff of the root beer from the mug. "Annie's has to stay the same."

The food followed, and they dug into the dinner. Amanda

gulped her hot dog in less than a minute and a half. She was starving from not having eaten for most of the day.

When they'd finished, she went and paid for both of them at the cash register.

"You didn't have to do that," said Tyler, when she'd returned.

"I wanted to."

"Then I'm paying for mini-golf."

Smee's Mini Golf was another Lake Batonkin original. It'd been built in the early nineteen-fifties, eighteen holes of moderately challenging putt-putt golf. It hadn't changed a whit since. It had been added to the register of state historic sites when they were children.

Amanda knew every hole by heart, and so did Tyler. Their matchups had been intense, and now they picked up right where they left off.

"I got you," said Tyler.

"Don't even think about it," she replied.

The game was on. Amanda took an early lead on the doghouse, but Tyler came roaring back on the anthill. Tinny classic guitar rock that played from the speakers mounted around the course.

Later, the flattop added a few strokes to both their scores. Then Tyler scored a hole in one on the wishing well. Amanda shook her head in frustration. She'd never been good at that one.

At the end of the course, she put the ball in the second ring for par 2, and he did the same. Final score: Amanda 39, Tyler 37.

She handed him the scorecard. "You could frame it," she said.

"I've done better," he said.

"But you get to play all the time."

"Twice a week. I have a frequent player card."

She joshed him in the shoulder. So far it hadn't felt like a date, which was fine with her. It was two friends reacquainting themselves.

"Where to?" she said.

"You know where," he said.

Lake Batonkin Ice Cream was housed in a geodesic dome across the street from the mini golf. The owners had plastered their menu willy-nilly all over the outside panels, no rhyme or reason. Amanda suspected they weren't all there, mentally.

As they stood in line, Tyler voiced a similar thought. "I wonder how much longer they're gonna keep it together here."

"It's still that old couple?" asked Amanda.

"Yeah, and they're ancient now."

She peered at the random bits of menu taped up on the outside walls of the dome. "Wow. It's even more impossible than it was before."

"My mom knows them and she won't set foot in their house," Tyler said.

"I bet."

At the window, Amanda crouched down slightly so her voice would go through the small slat. "One small pistachio cone, please."

"And a large banana split," added Tyler.

They paid, and the desserts came up surprisingly quickly at the next window.

"Come on," said Tyler, "let's head to the pier."

Nine pm, and the sun was finally setting over the lake.

Amanda followed her childhood friend up the ramp and out to the end of the pier. Water lapped softly against the pilings. Seagulls cawed lazily from overhead.

Amanda licked her ice cream cone. Tyler leaned against the railing next to her.

"Pretty good that we've made it this far without talking about it," he said.

She stiffened. "Yeah, it's good to be good at something."

"You ever go to her grave?"

Amanda licked her ice cream cone and shook her head no.

"Me neither," he said. "She's right over there." He gestured towards the town cemetery.

"I know where it is," said Amanda.

He took a large bite of his banana split. Then: "You ever think about how things could've turned out differently?"

Amanda waited to reply. "I couldn't kiss anybody for a long time," she finally said. "Sometimes when someone tries to kiss me, and I'm not ready…. I just freeze."

"Yeah," he said.

"I think I met her dad today," she said.

"Elsie's?"

"Yeah."

"Where were you?"

"Out at Handley's Market."

"What were you doin' out there?"

"Asking questions. I'm an investigator."

"Did he recognize you?"

"Yep."

"What did you say to him?"

"Nothing. I left."

He used his plastic spoon to push the ice cream around his paper dish. "He doesn't show himself much anymore. I think he just hangs with his fishing buddies."

Amanda felt panic stirring inside of her. It didn't matter

how pleasant it was here on this pier. Something compelled her to take shelter.

"I have to leave," she stammered, "but it's been great seeing you."

"Amanda, wait—"

She was already off, down the pier. Tyler pursued her for a few steps, then stopped and watched her run off.

Chapter Fourteen

AMANDA HAD RETURNED to Lake Batonkin for work, but the town wasn't known for its remote work-friendly policies.

There were only three cafes, and two of them didn't even have tables: they were takeout only. Amanda had tried working at the third one, The Coffee Mill, but a sign on the wall had made it clear that she wasn't supposed to be there for more than an hour. She'd stayed two hours and left, feeling guilty.

Then she'd rediscovered the Lake Batonkin Public Library.

It lay on a back road, near where the old Air Force base had been located until its closure in the late nineteen-eighties. It was a midcentury one-story structure, with a large reading room on one end, and a used bookstore at the other end, which was full of hardbacks that the library director decided were unimportant enough to continue taking up space on the shelving.

Amanda had gone there a few times as a child, and now she found that the reading room was set up perfectly for her work. Every morning, after swimming in the lake, she showered and bought a cup of dark roast from the Coffee Mill. Then she drove out to the library and set up at the same table.

The ladies who worked at the checkout desk greeted her. "Good morning, Amanda," said one. She was heavy, dyed her hair burgundy, and was probably the sweetest person Amanda had ever met. Her name was Dorothy.

"Good morning, Dorothy," Amanda returned.

Next to her was a thin woman with knitted eyebrows and eyes widened in a way that she'd just seen something very disturbing. That was Karen.

"Hi Karen," said Amanda.

The librarian's eyes flicked over to her. "Yeah."

That was the best Amanda could hope for. Karen had a shortage of social skills. That was a problem when her job required that she work with the public.

On the floor of the library were scattered several old-fashioned claw bathtubs. Each one was filled with pillows and painted a different color: red, blue, yellow, green. She'd loved those tubs as a child. She'd come here on rainy days and lost herself in books. At the time, she'd read every book about sea creatures that the library offered.

This morning, Amanda sat down at her customary table and arranged her laptop and began to write her report. She'd amassed a lot of data, some anecdotal evidence, and some witness testimony.

"Amanda dear," said a voice, "how is everything?"

She looked up. It was Dorothy. She was standing there, slightly hunched, her hands folded over themselves modestly at her belt buckle, as if trying to hide her body.

"Fine," said Amanda, "what's up?"

"Do you know about the fundraiser for the WLBR television newscast tonight?"

"No," said Amanda.

"I think you should come. Violet Carruthers is celebrating her fifth year on the air, and a lot of important people are going to be there. You might make some new friends."

"Thank you, maybe I will," she said.

The lady smiled sweetly. "It's at the Bird's Nest at seven o'clock."

Amanda thanked the woman and returned to her report. That would be an event she shouldn't miss.

At seven o'clock that night, Amanda entered the Bird's Nest. She was wearing a pair of jeans, a cute flouncy top, and a pair of new sneakers. Her hair was pulled back with a banana clip that she'd found since the other side.

A young man waited at a folding table. He had a gray metal box for money and a row of pin buttons. Amanda assumed he was an intern.

Then he lifted his face. She recognized him. It was Logan Kent, the young sidekick news anchor.

"Hello and welcome to the WLBR fundraiser," Logan said.

"You're Logan, right? You're the news anchor! Why do they have you collecting money at the front?"

"I don't know," he said. He looked frustrated, then muttered, "I'm going back to college this fall, so whatever."

"I'm Amanda, by the way."

"Nice to meet you." He shook her hand. "So, entry is fifty dollars."

Amanda winced. She didn't make much money in her government job, but she could make an exception this one time. Besides, it was a fundraiser. She probably should've been prepared to turn over some money.

She handed him a fifty-dollar bill, and he reverently laid it in the silver box. "Beautiful," he said. In turn he handed her a "My Name is…" sticker, plus a button.

"The drinks are over by the wall," said Logan, "and the snacks are outside on the patio. Enjoy yourself!"

He turned to the next guests. Amanda walked into the main room and took a glass of white wine from the drinks table. The room was mostly empty. Through the glass she saw the packed veranda. It was too beautiful an evening to be cooped up inside.

She passed outside onto the veranda overlooking the lake. They'd removed the tables and all the attendees were out here, at least sixty so far. Many of the women were in cute sundresses, and the men wore polo shirts tucked into chino pants and loafers. It was a beautiful evening on Lake Batonkin, the sky a riot of pastels.

"Oh hey, it's Amanda!" a raspy voice shouted.

It was Lily, her landlord. She was wearing a dirty orange t-shirt and rolled up jean shorts with flip-flops. A glass of brown liquor dangled from her hand.

"Yes it is, Lily!"

"If I'd known you were coming, I woulda dressed up better!"

"You look fine," lied Amanda.

"Sure I do," she replied, "it took me three hours to doll this up." She took a swig of the drink. "Hey you're still expectin' that propane tank, right?"

"Yes," said Amanda, annoyed. "I can't cook anything without it."

"Well, it's gonna take a bit longer. They can't get the tanks out for at least another week."

Amanda shrugged. "Whatever it takes."

"But I think I fixed the refrigerator this afternoon. Those old cabins got wiring problems like you wouldn't believe."

Lily's eyes lit up. "Hey, you want me to introduce you around? I know everybody here."

"That'd be great."

For the next twenty minutes, Lily took Amanda to different people. To Jim and Kathy, a couple who owned a water sports company. To Wayne and Teresa, a couple who owned an agriculture equipment store. To Sam and Christina, a couple who owned a small resort down the beach from Lily's.

It was a lot of white couples, and Amanda struggled to keep them all straight. The names were all similar, the ages were similar, and the clothing was similar. She never had the best memory for faces, and she struggled to find ways to differentiate them from one another.

"And now," said Lily, "you're gonna meet someone real special."

"Who's that?"

"The woman we're all here for! Violet Carruthers."

The broadcaster was perched lightly on the edge of a high stool in the corner of the veranda. She wore a flowing yellow gown that was entirely too formal for the event. Next to her, a shy, rotund man held her drink for her.

"Violet," said Lily, "I want you to meet Amanda. She's doing something big with the lake, some scientific stuff on the sand or I don't know what. Anyways, this is her!"

So much for a dignified introduction. Amanda stuck out her hand; Violet grasped it briefly.

"Charmed," the newscaster said.

"Likewise," said Amanda. "I enjoy your broadcasts very much."

"Thank you—that's very nice of you to say! What's your story, Amanda? Why are you here at Lake Batonkin?"

"I'm working on a report for the EPA about the mussel invasion in Lake Batonkin," said Amanda.

Violet tilted her head to the side. "Oh my goodness, that sounds important. Is this your first time?"

"No," she said, "I grew up every summer here."

"Oh, how wonderful," said Violet. She seemed to be play-acting a bit, but Amanda figured that she was always like that.

"Is this your husband?" said Amanda.

The shy man next to her nodded. "Chris Carruthers."

"Someone said you're a doctor?"

"Yes, I'm head of surgery at the hospital."

Violet was sizing up Amanda. Then she said, "You know, I'd like to do a remote piece about you."

"About me?" said Amanda.

"Oh absolutely! I can see it now—a young science detective returns to Lake Batonkin to solve a mystery!"

A science detective, Amanda thought. That was a funny way to describe her job, but it wasn't entirely wrong.

"I wouldn't say no," said Amanda.

"Terrific," said Violet. "Give me your phone number and I'll call you to set up a day and a time."

They exchanged phone numbers, and Violet promised to call.

Other people came forward for the chance to chat with the queen of Lake Batonkin news media, and Amanda felt herself bumped aside.

Chapter Fifteen

THE FIRST DRAFT of her mussels report was due in Stephen's inbox in less an hour, and Amanda was starting to panic.

It was short. Much too short.

Laying on her bed, Amanda's face was illuminated by the laptop screen. She wore her eyeglasses, the chunky ones with black frames that embarrassed her, the ones she never wore except in private.

The report was expected to be at least twenty pages. She had eleven pages and wasn't sure what else to include. She'd included all of her data on hand, interview quotes, and some analysis.

There had to be more. But there wasn't any more, at least not right now.

Crap.

An email popped up on her screen. It was from her boss, Stephen Grandulet.

Need that report ASAP, Amanda.

She sighed, hit reply, attached the document, and typed a response.

I've got eleven pages and thank you for the reminder!! Here it is. - Amanda

Then she hit send. The email whisked away, across the ether, into the inbox of the man who controlled her future. Her kind but professional boss.

She hoped that he would view her as equally professional.

Amanda closed her laptop and rolled onto her back and rubbed her eyes. They were nearly crossed from all the screen work she'd been doing the last two days.

She needed to take the night off.

On her nightstand was the local newspaper. It was a weekly circular, one of the last of its kind. Sixteen small pages filled with local advertising, astrological horoscopes, comic strips, some real estate advertorials, and a handful of local-interest articles.

On the back was a small advertisement: *Lake Batonkin Cinema—half off Wednesday nights*! Under Now Playing was listed a romantic comedy that had caught Amanda's eye earlier in the summer, on a billboard in Chicago.

That sounded just right.

She got dressed. Then, just to be sure, she checked the refrigerator. Lily said she'd fixed it.

It was still warm inside. Lily hadn't fixed anything.

Amanda put it out of her mind. She put her shoes on and left the cabin.

The old Lake Batonkin Cinema stood downtown, a reminder of how important the movies used to be. In the old days, even small towns had miniature movie palaces built in their commercial centers, and this was one of them. The theater featured elaborate scrollwork on the outside, and a single ticket window that had been painted to look like a fancy old window from centuries ago.

Amanda remembered the cinema, but she hadn't been here since that final, tragic summer.

An elderly woman in a modest orange cardigan sweater waited behind the glass.

"One ticket for *Bridge to Love*," said Amanda.

The woman looked up at her. "Just one?"

"Yes."

"You're coming alone to this movie?"

"Yes."

"You sure you don't want two tickets?"

Amanda rolled her eyes. "Do you see anybody else with me?"

The woman held up her palms. "All right, all right. Five dollars."

Amanda paid in cash and received a ticket. She entered the small lobby. A concession stand waited, empty. An old popcorn machine was lit up nicely. Amanda looked around for a moment, waiting for someone to help her.

The door of the ticket booth cracked open. The old woman stuck her head out. "You want something?"

"A small popcorn."

The woman sighed. She hobbled out, went behind the concession stand, and filled up a small cup with popcorn. "Three dollars," she said.

Amanda paid her a second time.

"Thank you," said Amanda.

Saying nothing, the woman went back into the ticket booth and shut the door.

The theater featured sconces on the walls and a heavy red velvet curtain covering the screen. It was empty except for one other couple. Amanda took a seat two rows behind them and sank down into the cushion. It was thick and luxurious.

She ate her popcorn and waited for the movie to begin. Nobody else came into the theater. She let her brain empty itself.

When she'd finished her popcorn, she checked her phone. It was already ten minutes past the start time.

Then the old woman came down the aisle. "I'm sorry, folks, I can't play the movie tonight."

She was apparently the projectionist as well.

"Why not?" said Amanda.

"I need at least eight guests to run the film. You guys are only three, and I'll lose money. Come up front for your refund."

Amanda felt disappointed, but this was how it went in Lake Batonkin. She stood up and went back into the lobby and took her refund from the old lady and went outside.

The night was cool and cloudy, so she decided against taking a walk on the beach or getting an ice cream.

Across the street from the theater was the Woodbridge Tavern. The exterior walls were built of pine, no surprise there. The sign featured a cartoon beaver holding a pint of beer.

In the parking lot, Amanda noticed several motorcycles parked. Not casual small ones, or Japanese street racers, but Harley-Davidsons. The type that blatted loud enough to be heard two towns over.

Why not, she thought. She could order a beer, zone out, and then go home.

She entered the tavern. The interior walls and tables were made of pine. A group of gnarly bikers stood around a pool table, sticks in hand. They had beards and wore leather coats. They noticed her right away.

Amanda went to the other side of the room and planted herself on a stool at the bar. A young woman not too much older than herself came over, a rag thrown across her shoulder.

"What are you havin'," she said.

"A beer," said Amanda.

"Which one?"

"What do you have on tap?"

She shook her head. "We got bottles."

"Then I don't know. Give me a lager."

"We got Miller or Bud Lite."

Those were both lagers, but Amanda decided not to make a big deal about it. "Miller," she said.

The woman gave her a bottle of Miller, no glass. She drank from it and arranged her elbows on the counter and fixed her eyes on a beaver made of neon lights behind the bar.

"Darlin, I hope this stool isn't taken," a man said.

She turned. A large biker was slipping his bulk next to her. His black leather smelled like old sunscreen and his black boots had three-inch heels. His face and hands were sunburned.

"You can sit where you want," she replied.

"Seems like you're up for the summer," he said.

"Does it?"

"Yeah. You got city girl written all over you."

"I'm staying here for a while," she responded.

The bartender brought him a beer. "I used to know this yoga teacher, she was so flexible. She could do amazing things with her body. I used to just sit back and watch her."

Amanda lifted an eyebrow. This guy had creep written all over him.

"Why did you just tell me that?" she said.

"She kinda looked like you."

"I don't do yoga."

"Maybe you oughta try." He winked at her.

At that moment, her phone lit up with a call. The screen read Environmental Protection Agency. It was a 312 number. She recognized that number.

It was Stephen, her boss.

"Excuse me," she said, standing up. She left cash on the bar and hightailed it out the door.

Outside on the sidewalk, she answered the call and put it on speakerphone. She held the phone horizontally up near her mouth.

"Hello?" she said.

"Amanda, it's Stephen." His voice sounded tense.

"Hey there," she said.

He cut to the chase. "So this report isn't complete. I know it's a first draft but you've just scratched the surface of what's going on. What's happening? You've had weeks up there."

"I know, it's just that—"

"People aren't talking?"

"They are," she said, "but maybe it's not the right people."

"You're going to the locals? Like we discussed?"

"Of course."

His voice grew serious. "Listen, if you're getting distracted by summer memories, I can recall you to Chicago and send somebody else."

"No," she said, pacing in nervous circles, "please, it's not that. I just need more time. I'm trying some new strategies."

"Like what?"

An incoming text message lit up her screen. It was from Violet Carruthers.

Interview this week?

Amanda felt a thrill of excitement shoot up her body. "I'm going on local television."

"To talk about the mussels?" he said.

"Yes," she replied. "They want to interview me."

"I'll have to run it by public affairs first."

"Just give me more time up here," she pleaded.

He paused. "For professional or personal reasons, Amanda?"

"Professional, Stephen," she said, trying to convince herself it was the truth.

"All right," he said. "You stay a few more weeks, we'll reimburse. And I'll email you more thoughts about the report tomorrow."

"Thank you," she said.

"Enjoy a S'more at a beach bonfire for me. Bye."

He hung up. Amanda looked at her phone, filled with contradictory emotions.

"Hey!" shouted a voice.

She looked up. It was the creep from the bar. "Come back on biker night if you wanna get up to no good!"

"Thank you!" she said, giving him a thumbs-up, though she really wanted to give him a different finger.

Amanda turned and walked down the sidewalk quickly. Two thoughts were pinging around inside her head. One was that she was never returning to that bar. The second was that she hadn't really wanted to leave this place.

She pulled out her phone and replied to Violet Carruthers.

Chapter Sixteen

AMANDA AND VIOLET agreed to meet at eleven o'clock Friday morning for the interview. They settled upon the downtown beach next to the pier, a convenient place to film owing to the facilities and the parking.

On the morning of the interview, Amanda woke up to a message from Stephen that she'd obtained permission from the public affairs office. She glanced briefly at the attached agreement but she was too anxious to read it.

Instead, Amanda began to agonize over her wardrobe. She went through all seven of her outfits but couldn't decide on any of them. She decided instead upon an emergency shopping trip to the clothing store.

Clamanto's Women's Apparel had been a staple of the community for over half a century, but Amanda hadn't been inside until now.

It was an old store, and the employees were even older. Amanda moved through the racks. She was disappointed. There were shoulder-pad business suits that seemed to have been hanging there since the nineteen-eighties. There were muumuus that she was far too young to wear. There were modest cardigans and simple ten-dollar short-sleeve tops.

Amanda shook her head. This had been a mistake. She shouldn't have come here.

She stepped outside and walked to another women's apparel store, Genevieve's Fashion. It wasn't open. A sign on the door said it was closed for the next two weeks for vacation. Amanda wondered why any business owner in Lake Batonkin would close during the summer, when the population of the town swelled by thousands. But the people here moved to their own rhythms.

"Amanda!" she heard a voice call.

It was Violet Carruthers. She was stepping out of a car, dressed in a red sport coat and matching red lipstick. Behind her, Logan was in shorts and flip-flops, holding a video camera.

"Hi Violet," said Amanda. "You're almost an hour early."

"I know," she said, "but I was just so excited to learn about your project that I couldn't wait!" she cried, grabbing Amanda by the arm. "This is going to be my lead story on the broadcast tonight."

"Oh wow."

Violet cocked her head. "Aren't you excited?"

"It's just that I don't know what to wear," said Amanda.

"Oh," said the newscaster, "what you're wearing looks lovely."

Amanda looked down. She wore a plain spaghetti strap top in seafoam green, a pair of khaki shorts, and white running shoes with socks.

"Are you sure?"

"I'm sure. Just wear that!"

"Okay."

"Besides, does anyone know what an EPA person usually looks like?"

"Sunburned," Amanda said.

Violet laughed. "Save that for on-camera! What a good response!" She cast an arm across Amanda's shoulders. "Let's go down to the beach and get set up."

The camera was placed on a tripod in the sand. Logan then set up a small generator and connected three lights. Amanda didn't know why they needed extra lighting on a sunny day on the beach. She also wondered why they were making the college intern news anchor double as a tech person.

Violet read her mind. "The artificial lights will soften the natural sunlight," she said.

"I see," said Amanda.

"Do you want to come with me to the bathroom? We should check our makeup."

"I don't know—"

"Listen to me," she said. "You *need* to check your makeup."

Message delivered. Violet slung her makeup case over her shoulder and took Amanda's hand and pulled her across the sand towards the changing room. Inside, mothers and daughters were running around in wet swimsuits and towels. The two women stood over a sink and shared the same mirror.

Violet adjusted her eyeliner, then turned to Amanda and studied her face. "You're going to need some foundation."

"I'm not really good at this."

"Then let me help." The newscaster began applying foundation to Amanda's face. "This will do you a world of good."

"I'm representing the public sector. It's not a sexy career."

Violet ignored her and applied eyeliner and lipstick. Then she stepped back. "You look terrific. Lovely."

Amanda glanced in the mirror. She barely recognized herself.

———

They set up two folding chairs under the lights. Violet sat primly, with strict posture. Amanda sat more relaxedly, hands folded in her lap, legs crossed.

Behind them, the waters of Lake Batonkin rippled. A group of children splashed in the water.

They'd already shot what they called the B-roll, the supplementary footage that Amanda wouldn't be speaking in. They'd done a minute of Amanda standing at water's edge. They'd done a couple minutes of her strolling down the beach. They'd done several angles of her hands holding a small pile of the invasive mussels.

"Ready?" said Logan.

"No," said Violet. She produced a handheld mirror and studied herself. It was the fourth time she'd adjusted her face. Amanda couldn't tell a difference.

"We have to be back by two o'clock," he said.

"If we must," she mumbled, snapping the mirror shut.

The college student brought out a tiny microphone on a clip, its cord trailing across the sand towards his equipment. Amanda looked down and affixed it to her blouse. He did the same for Amanda.

"This is so exciting," Violet said. "I never get to do remote segments. The owner won't let me."

"Who's the owner?" said Amanda, knowing the answer.

"My husband."

Amanda didn't say anything to that.

"How's the audio?" said Violet.

Logan gave her a thumbs up.

"Let's check one more time." Violet placed one hand on

her stomach, held the other one out, and proceeded to trill through a series of *do-re-mi-fa-so-la-ti-do*. She had a small, fluted voice that sounded like a fork clinking against a champagne glass.

It grabbed the attention of everybody on the beach. Heads turned.

"That was lovely," said Amanda.

"I've been training for years," she said.

"Do you perform?"

"Only at home for the dogs," said Violet, "but this winter I've been invited to audition for a performance in Alpena at the community theater."

"Congratulations," said Amanda.

"It is quite an honor. Now, let's begin. Logan, are we ready?"

"We've been ready this whole time," came the reply.

"Don't get fresh with me."

He ignored her. "Okay, we're rolling in three, two..."

He lowered his arm to indicate that they were now ready to go. Violet put on her broadcaster's voice. "Good afternoon, I'm sitting here with Amanda Baylor, a science detective sent by the federal government to Lake Batonkin this summer. She's investigating the arrival of the donkey mussels into our very valuable but fragile ecosystem." She turned to Amanda. "Thanks for being here, Amanda."

"You're welcome," said Amanda. "Also, they're called zebra mussels."

"Oh goodness," said Violet, "I'm sorry!"

"No problem." Amanda decided not to remind her that her last name was Taylor, not Baylor.

"So tell us—how dangerous are these little mussels?"

Amanda explained her position at the EPA, then the agency's task to protect the waterways of the country. She talked about the economic impact that the zebra mussels could have upon the region. She described the previous mussels, and how they impacted the entire world.

"That is very interesting! Is there anything we can do to help?"

That was the moment Amanda was waiting for. It was why she'd agreed to this interview. "Yes—if anybody has any information or ideas about how to combat the zebra mussels, please email me! I'm writing a report that's due soon. You can also find me most days at the Lake Batonkin Public Library."

Violet beamed towards her. "That's wonderful. Thank you, Amanda."

"You're welcome, Violet."

The newscaster turned to the camera. "Reporting from the downtown municipal beach, I'm Violet Carruthers."

They remained still for another moment until Logan said, "Cut."

Then Violet disengaged her microphone. Her manner changed. "I do not like being corrected on camera, Amanda."

"I'm sorry, but—"

"You made me look terrible!"

Amanda felt herself lose her temper. "Donkey mussels don't exist, Violet! Aren't you a journalist? You're supposed to be accurate!"

Violet stood up and huffed. "Whatever makes you feel important, young lady." The cameraman theatrically handed the newscaster her purse; she snatched it. "Let's get back to the studio, Logan."

As she walked away, Amanda cupped her hands to her mouth. "And my last name is Taylor, not Baylor!"

The temperamental news anchor didn't reply. Amanda looked down at Logan, who was winding up the electrical cord. "Can you believe this?"

"Unfortunately, I can."

"So you're just trying to get through the summer."

"Pretty much." He paused, then: "Give me your email address and I'll make sure that it gets onscreen."

"Promise?"

"Yeah, I'll do it myself. Promise."

Amanda scribbled it on a notecard and handed it to him. "Thank you," she said.

Chapter Seventeen

AT FIVE MINUTES to eleven that night, Amanda paced anxiously in her cabin. The television was already tuned to WLBR. A local commercial for a water park on the other side of the state was playing.

She heard a knock at the door. She opened it and saw Lily, bottle of whiskey dangling from her hand. She was teetering in her flip-flops.

"Hey sweetie," she said, "how's that refrigerator working now?"

Amanda tilted her head, confused. "You said that you fixed it, but you didn't."

"I thought I did." She paused. "Oh wait—I think I went in the wrong cabin!" She guffawed.

Amanda pinched the bridge of her nose between her thumb and forefinger. She closed her eyes. "Lily..."

"Well, pin a tail on my butt and call me a donkey," said Lily. "I'll take care of that, right away."

Amanda let her inside. Lily pushed past her and opened the fridge. "I'm gonna have to get into the wiring just like I did on the other cabin."

"Can it wait until tomorrow?" said Amanda.

"I guess. Hey, what's this?"

The landlord picked up the jar of peanut butter and jelly that Amanda had been using to feed herself. The bread sat nearby.

"It's exactly what it looks like. PB and J. Do you want one?" With her erratic landlord, Amanda found it was easier just to ride the horse in the direction it was already going.

"Hell no," Lily said. "I can't stand peanut butter. I fed it to my cat for years and I think that's what killed her before her time."

"How old was she?"

"Sixteen," she said.

None of that made any sense, but then Amanda forgot all about the conversation, because the tinny trumpeting welcome song on the television announced the start of the newscast.

She sat on the bed, cross-legged. "Lily, you have to either leave or sit down," she said, "because the news is on."

"So you're a big fan now! I knew it!"

"Actually, I'm on the broadcast tonight."

Lily fell back into the only chair in the room. "Well! This oughta be good."

As promised, her interview was in fact the lead story. Violet sat primly behind the desk. She wore an emerald blouse beneath a large white sport coat. Gaudy costume jewelry hung from her neck and wrists. Logan sat next to her in the same father's sport coat that he always wore.

"Welcome to the WLBR eleven o'clock news, I'm Violet Carruthers," she said. Then she tossed her hair. "It may come as a surprise, but not everybody who comes to our community for the summer season is on vacation. One young lady, Amanda Baylor, is a science detective from the Environmental Protection Agency, and she's here investigating a new mussel invasion. Let's find out what she had to say."

Amanda watched the broadcast through her fingers. The B-reel showed her walking along the beach, holding the mussels, chatting on the beach with Violet. The interview scenes were a bit too up close for her taste. All together, the piece lasted nearly three minutes. The chyron below the screen read *Amanda Taylor, Environmental Protection Agency*. That was Logan, looking out for her last name. Unfortunately, viewers were unlikely to read the correction.

Now the whole town was going to get Amanda's last name wrong. But at least they aired the portion of the interview where she asked the town to email her information. Logan came through again, displaying her address in clear, bold letters on the bottom of the screen.

When the segment ended, Lily took a swig from her bottle. "Girl, you're gonna be famous around here now."

Amanda breathed out a sigh of relief and flopped on the bed.

"You think?"

"Oh, everybody's gonna be talkin' about you. I better hire us some security."

She cackled at her own joke. Then Lily poured some whiskey into a small juice glass and handed it to Amanda. They clinked.

"Cheers," said Lily.

"Cheers," replied Amanda. "To Lake Batonkin."

A few minutes later, after Lily stumbled out the door, Amanda stared at the ceiling until very late in the night.

Next morning, a knock at the door woke up Amanda with a start.

"Not now, Lily," she shouted, irritated.

A man's voice said, "It's me. Tyler."

She bolted up in bed. What was he doing here?

Amanda stumbled to the door and flung it open. He stood there, a tall silhouette against the morning blue sparkle of the lake.

Tyler Boyd.

He was holding a brown bag and a pair of coffees in a tray. "Is this a bad time?"

"I mean, it's not ideal," she said. Her eyes went down to her dirty sleep crop top and baggy sleep pants. "How did you find out where I was?"

"I asked around. People said you were here. Then Lily told me which one was your cabin."

Amanda frowned. Was her landlord giving out her cabin number to anybody who showed up? Maybe getting a security guard was a good idea.

"So what do you need?"

"Today is gonna be a crazy day for you, and I thought you might want some breakfast."

He handed her the brown bag. Inside were two ham-cheese-and-egg breakfast biscuits.

She looked up. "You saw the news?"

Tyler nodded. "You did good. I was impressed." He nodded towards the lake. "Why don't you get dressed and we can eat at the picnic table down the way?"

Amanda thought about it. She didn't have anything to lose. "Give me ten minutes."

The biscuit felt still warm in Amanda's hand as she sat herself at the old picnic table.

The wooden picnic table was just off the sand, in a small

grove of birch trees. The table had been there for years, and nobody knew who the owner was. It didn't matter anymore. The low growth tickled against Amanda's legs.

Across from her, Tyler sat sideways on the other bench, one leg under the table, the other splayed out against the sand. His right arm rested on the table, his fingers drumming on the surface of the weather-beaten wood.

She took a bite of the breakfast biscuit. "This was really nice of you," she said, mouth half full.

"I wanted to lure you out for a few minutes before the whole town starts trying to talk to you."

"Do you think they will?

He scratched his head. "Your profile has definitely gone up."

Amanda scrunched up her nose. That could be good or bad. She knew what happened to people who became famous, either accidentally or on purpose.

"Well, I need some help. These mussels are tough to crack."

"No pun intended."

She shot him a finger pistol. "Nice. Seriously, though, it could hurt my career if I don't get this thing done."

"I'm going to abruptly change topics," he said. "Is that okay?"

She went on high alert. "Um, okay?"

"My mother wanted me to give you something," he said.

Tyler reached into his bag and produced a plastic Ziploc bag. Inside was a small stack of photos.

"What's this?"

"After that first day you came into the store, she went searching for you in our family photo albums."

"Oh my God—"

"You're in every photo in this stack, in some way. These are all prints, for you to keep."

Amanda covered her mouth in surprise. She watched her trembling fingers reach into the bag and pull out the photos.

The first one was her and Tyler, ages nine or ten. Posing with arms out on the beach, same straight up-and-down bodies, making huge toothy smiles with their eyes shut.

"Look at that," she said.

She looked at another one. She and an older boy were on a canoe together.

"It's Joey," she said, a note of joy slipping into her throat. "He was so much fun! Where is he?"

"He moved to Wisconsin to work for a dairy company."

She flipped to another photo. "And look—that girl, the one with the glasses, she kept telling us something was 'in Shane' but nobody knew who Shane was—"

"—and it took us forever to realize that she had a speech impediment—"

"—she was trying to say *this was insane*—"

Amanda laughed hard, a tear coursing down her cheek. She was enveloped in the thick haze of past. It smelled sweet.

Then she found the next photo, and that feeling disappeared. Her breath was sucked out of her body.

"Oh God," she said. "Oh God."

"What?" Tyler craned his head and saw the photo. His face darkened. "Oh shoot. I told my mom not to put that one in."

Three people in this photo: Amanda, Tyler, and a thin blonde girl. She had braces and a pink swimsuit and looked like an awkward bird in that preteen way. She looked like she could've been somebody.

"Elsie," Amanda said. The word came out choked.

"Elsie," repeated Tyler.

Amanda studied the photo, hand over mouth. "I forgot how pretty she was."

"Yeah."

Tyler turned and pointed out to the water just in front of the cape. "It was right over there."

Amanda didn't say anything. She studied the photo for a while longer, feeling all the feelings bubbling up to the surface. It wasn't what she wanted, not at this very moment, but it was happening regardless.

"Changing the topic," said Tyler, "do you remember the fourth of July we spent at this table?"

Amanda's head jerked up. "No. Should I remember that?"

"You've been gone a while."

"Who were we with?" Her eyes roved the sky looking for answers.

"My brother Henry, and that Carlotti family. Remember? We put the bottle rockets right here on the table—"

Her eyes lit up. "And that one caught on fire when we weren't looking—"

"—and shot off the picnic table between you and that old lady—"

They both doubled over in laughter.

"Oh god," she said, smiling. Amanda looked through the remainder of the photos and handed them over. "That was really nice. Thank you for bringing them."

"You're welcome."

His large hand closed over hers for a brief moment. Amanda looked up at him. Tyler was looking at her with a curious expression on his face, as though there were something more he wanted to say, but he was holding back.

He stood up and moved around the table towards her. He crouched next to her so that his face was on par with her own. His fingers lifted her chin towards him.

Amanda knew where this was headed. She got that old squirrelly feeling inside. It happened whenever she was about to kiss somebody. It's why she avoided it as much as possible.

"Again, thank you so much," she said, "but I have to go."

"Crazy day coming up?" he said, releasing her chin.

"Yeah."

He rose to his feet. "Okay, I'll walk you back."

They moved back down the sand together. When Tyler took her hand again, she didn't complain. And when he took off in his truck, she quietly watched him go.

Chapter Eighteen

AT THE LIBRARY THAT MORNING, Amanda found her email inbox filled with twenty-three new messages. All of them had subject lines that said things like *Saw you on the news last night* or *Zebra mussels ruined my husband's boat*.

She seated herself at a table tucked away behind some shelves. She wanted privacy. Then she began to answer the inquiries, one by one, via email. She offered her phone number to each of them, if they should want to talk.

As she did so, within minutes, her phone started ringing. It seemed that more people watched the news than she'd anticipated. She quickly put it on vibrate and answered the calls, one by one. Though she was sitting far away from any other patron, she still tried to speak in a low voice. It was a library, after all.

Soon Amanda sensed a presence at her side. It was Karen, the pinched and mean librarian.

"I'm sorry, we cannot have you talking like this in here," she said sorrowfully.

Amanda felt guilt knitting her intestines into little

shameful booties. "I'm sorry. Is there a private room I can use?"

"We don't have the private study rooms anymore," she said. "We got rid of them last year."

"So where can I go?"

Karen sighed and thought about it. "I don't know."

Dorothy, the friendly librarian, came up behind her. "Amanda, maybe you want to sit outside on the grass, under the tree? You can talk all you want and still use the wifi from there. Does that sound okay?"

Amanda thought about it. It was better than nothing.

"Okay," she said.

"I'll bring you a chair."

Karen shot an angry glance at Dorothy, then huffed off back to the desk.

Soon Amanda was parked on a folding chair beneath the oak tree outside the library's front doors. She held her computer in her lap. Through the branches, the yellow sunlight dappled against the screen on her laptop, making it hard to read. She had to lift it up to her face to make out some of the words on the email messages.

The phone calls kept pouring in. During the few minutes it took for her to use the bathroom, go outside, and set up the folding chair, three more voicemails had appeared on her phone.

Over the next few hours, she fielded phone calls from old people, young people, timid people, loudmouths, lunatics. Some people called her just wanting to talk. One elderly man asked her out on a date and asked her if she minded that he was on an oxygen tank.

Amanda opened a spreadsheet and began to track all the

emails and calls. She put their names, ages, occupations, email address, phone numbers, and information offered. Then she added a column about follow-up.

At two pm, Dorothy came outside carrying a paper cup of lemonade and a chocolate chip cookie wrapped in a napkin. "We thought you must be thirsty," she said, "so here's a little snack."

Amanda looked up. She hadn't even noticed the time, or her hunger. "Thank you," she said.

"Folks are real friendly around here," said Dorothy. "You must be getting more tips than you know what to do with!"

"Isn't that the truth. Some of them don't even have anything to offer."

"People get lonely," the woman replied. "Any chance to talk to a stranger, they'll take it."

"You'd know better than anybody," said Amanda, nodding towards the library. "Working at the front desk."

Dorothy nodded. "You'd better believe it."

The library door opened. Karen appeared, her face more pinched than usual. She cupped her hands around her mouth and shouted: "Did you remind her about closing time?"

"No," Dorothy shouted back, "but I will."

"What do you have to tell me?" said Amanda.

"Just as a reminder, today we close at three."

"I thought you closed at six."

"We have a staff training today from three to six," she said.

"Crap," said Amanda. She still had nine phone calls to make, and three more emails had popped up in the last five minutes. "Well, thank you for telling me. I'll be sure to wrap it up."

For the next hour, she worked at lightning speed. Amanda tried not to be curt with potential people on the phone, but she was trying to cycle through them as quickly as possible. Still, some people just wanted to take their time, chatting familiarly as though Amanda were an old friend they hadn't seen in a couple years.

At five minutes to three, Amanda saw Karen motioning curtly to her from the library entrance. It was time to bring back the chair.

She closed her laptop and stood up. Then her phone rang again. She held a wait-a-minute index finger up to Karen while she answered the call.

"Amanda Taylor," she said.

"I know your name, young lady," a woman's voice said. "I gave birth to you."

Amanda froze in her tracks. "Mom?"

"I see someone doesn't look at her caller ID."

"I'm really busy right now—can I call you back?"

"No, don't bother," she said. "I'll just meet you for dinner tonight at the Bird's Nest."

"Seriously? Wait, are you here?"

"Well, I'm on the road," her mother said. "Meet me at seven-thirty. Love you dear."

The call ended. Her mother had hung up. Amanda stood there, looking at her phone, dumbfounded. Karen walked over to her and snatched the chair from her hand and carried it back inside, without a word.

"Thank you," Amanda called out sarcastically.

"We're closed!" shouted Karen, as the door shut.

Chapter Nineteen

WHEN AMANDA ARRIVED fifteen minutes early at the Bird's Nest, her mother was already seated at a table. She wore expensive leather sandals, capri pants, and a turquoise V-neck top. A whiskey cocktail was stuck to her hand.

"Hello dear," said her mother, rising.

Amanda gave her an obligatory hug, then sat down opposite.

"You look well," she said.

"I feel well."

"No," said her mother, "you feel good. If you feel well, that means you're skilled at the art of feeling."

Amanda tried not to roll her eyes. "How did you find out I was up here?"

"Somebody sent me the news clip. So I decided you were having too much fun and you needed a mother to harass you."

"That's nice of you," said Amanda.

Her mother dabbed at her mouth with a napkin, careful to fold it over the lipstick mark. "You could've told me you were coming here, you know."

"Why?"

"Because mothers like to know things."

"You went to Germany for two weeks last year without telling me."

"That was for business."

"So is this."

Her mother sighed. "Well, I'm not in my mid-twenties."

Amanda crinkled her forehead. "You had *me* in your mid-twenties. All I did was go back to the same lake where we went my whole life."

"Okay, I don't want to fight. You can see this anyway you'd like. Let's order some dinner—I'm starving."

She signaled to the waitress, who came over. It was Candace, the older woman who'd remembered Amanda's family on her first visit here.

"Hello Lisa," she said.

Startled, Amanda's mother looked up at the older woman. "Candace?"

"That's me," she said.

Amanda's mother clapped her hands. "You're still here? At the Birds' Nest, all this time!"

"Yes, ma'am," said Candace. "I was real sorry to hear about Carl when he passed."

"Oh, we'd been split up already," said Amanda's mother.

"But it's still hard, right? I mean, he was a fine man. You must have shared so many memories?"

"Of course," said her mother, shrugging, "if you say so." Then she brayed.

Amanda knew that laugh. It was her mom's public laugh, designed to attract attention. She'd been shrugging off her ex-husband's death since the day it happened. Her mother wasn't the sentimental type at all, and that was putting it mildly. Lisa Taylor was a career woman to the bone, currently vice-president of sales at an auto parts manufacturer downstate, her team responsible for over one hundred and fifty million dollars in sales revenue per year. It was a rare evening that saw her home before eight o'clock. She worked most Saturdays and spent Sundays prepping for the upcoming week. Her only hobby, as far as Amanda knew, was falling asleep in front of a reality television program holding a glass of brandy.

Why she'd agreed to marry Amanda's father all those years ago was anybody's guess. He'd been a man of quiet imagination, a sensitive soul who'd been happiest fishing here, on Lake Batonkin. In fact, he was the reason the family had come up every summer. Her parents hadn't been happy together, and they'd split up when Amanda was fourteen. Her dad had suffered a pair of strokes a couple of years later and died in Amanda's senior year of high school.

So they'd stopped coming up to Lake Batonkin, and Amanda had busied herself with trying to get past the memory of her father. She'd plunged into her science studies, her internships, her graduate school, now her career.

Just like her mother.

But Lake Batonkin had always stayed at the back of her head. She wasn't so sure if it'd stayed at the back of her mother's.

"So what're you ladies having?" said Candace.

"I'll take the perch," said Amanda.

"You do love it," the waitress said. "Sides?"

"Salad and fries."

"Ma'am?" she said, turning to Amanda's mother.

"I'll just have a plate of mixed vegetables."

Candace peered over her glasses. "That's it?"

"That'll be all."

The waitress collected their menus. "All right, I'll be back."

"Thanks," Amanda said.

The waitress disappeared, and her mother turned towards her. "It's been a lot of years since we were here."

"I know."

"What's it like being back in such a place?" Her mother looked around as though a chill had passed through her.

"It's not the best place for working," Amanda replied. "I've been going to the public library almost every day, but I can't make phone calls inside. I was sitting out on the lawn when you called."

Her mother fished the bright-red maraschino cherry out of her cocktail and placed it on the small bread plate. "That's something. Where are you staying?"

"Sunset Cottages."

"Oh dear. That's right near—"

She didn't finish the sentence. Amanda waited quietly. They didn't say anything for a minute.

"Is that crazy woman still running Sunset? Lola?"

"Lily."

Her mother smacked the table lightly. "Lily. How could I forget? What a loony tune."

"Yeah," said Amanda, "she's special."

"I don't know how you can tolerate being up here for so long. Your father was the only reason I came up here at all."

"I miss this place. It's the perfect definition of summer."

"To each her own," her mother said, shrugging.

Candace brought a basket of white bread with little individual butters strewn about. Amanda tried to slather the stuff on the bread, but the weak white bread broke under the cold butter. "Where are you staying, mom?"

"The MacArthur House," she said. Amanda detected a note of pride. It was the most expensive bed and breakfast in the area.

"I remember that place."

"Do you? You never stayed there! We couldn't afford that when you were a child."

"I remember the outside."

"Anyways," said her mother, "Lake Batonkin is something

I enjoyed when I was younger. But I wouldn't have visited here again, except to come see you."

"It reminds you of dad."

The plates of food were delivered, and Amanda stuffed her mouth with fried perch while listening to her mother rant.

"No," said her mother, "it's that they're uneducated. They're country people. Nobody here knows how to speak French, or—"

"You don't know how to speak French," said Amanda.

"That's incorrect," her mother said. "I've been taking French lessons. That's something you don't know about me, because we haven't been talking."

"Through an online course or something?"

"Yes. And I've been listening to AM radio from Quebec."

They went on like that, her mother detailing all the cultural activities that she's been pursuing for the last year that she hadn't told her daughter about. Amanda listened dutifully.

She finished her food and put her fork down. "Thank you for dinner, but I've got to get going. The whole town is trying to call me."

"I don't believe that."

"It's true. Look."

Amanda lifted her phone so her mother could read the screen: *14 voice messages*.

"Goodness," she said, "all right, work comes first. Don't let me hold you back."

"I won't," said Amanda.

"So what are we doing tomorrow?"

"I'm working."

"No, you're with me tomorrow," she said. "This is quality time with momma."

Amanda sighed. She couldn't say no. She would have to fit in work around her mother. "Okay, fine. What are we doing?"

"I've decided that we're going to the Lake Batonkin Museum."

Amanda hugged her mother around the shoulders, and they kissed on the cheeks. "Whatever you'd like."

"That is the correct response."

"And thanks for dinner!" Amanda said, walking away.

"Your mother raised you well!" she said.

Chapter Twenty

THE LAKE BATONKIN Museum was a ramshackle structure made of wooden boards painted a dark red. Pieces of iron farm equipment from the turn of the last century had been leaned against the outside wall, too big to carry inside.

Amanda's mother stood outside, hands on hips.

"I remember it being bigger," said Amanda, next to her.

"You were smaller," said her mother.

She felt annoyed in the same way she felt being dragged into a museum at age nine. "Do we have to go in here?"

"Yes, you do. It's what your mother wants."

"Fine."

"Just fine?"

"Great. I'm happy to be here."

Her voice was dripping with sarcasm. Her mother glared at her.

"Would you like to hold the door for your mother?"

Amanda held open the old-fashioned swinging door. They entered, and it banged behind them.

The museum was staffed by a single elderly volunteer. He was in his eighties and a blue nylon trucker's cap perched atop his bald dome announced that he'd served in the Vietnam War. His arms were crossed.

"Howdy," he said, nodding his head.

"Hi," said Amanda's mother.

"It's a two-dollar donation," he croaked. He lifted a gnarled hand and pointed at the donation jar.

"Here's ten," said Amanda's mother, stuffing it into the jar.

He didn't respond to the gift. "You start over there, by the glass exhibits, and circle around."

The size of a small house, the Lake Batonkin Museum was a near-fossil of a structure. Its floor was covered in a musty flattened green carpet. The original woodwork remained on the walls, dented and battered.

Amanda followed her mother through the exhibits. They looked at dioramas of the Lake Batonkin area as it appeared during the Ice Age. Somebody had placed two miniature indigenous people wearing loincloths atop a bed of white cotton. That was supposed to be snow.

"Where's the dinosaur," muttered Amanda.

"Hush now," her mother replied.

She turned. "I forgot to ask—how's Bradley doing?"

"Who?" said her mother.

"Your boyfriend?"

"I don't know who you're talking about."

Amanda understood the game her mother was playing. "How long ago did it happen?"

"Did what happen?" said her mother, entering the logging exhibit. A long double-handled saw was cutting through a plaster tree trunk. A life-sized cutout of Paul Bunyan hung from wall. Black-and-white photos of logging camps were arranged in old musty photo albums.

"The breakup. You guys must've broken up."

Her mother shook her head. "No, we never broke up, sweetheart, because we were never dating."

Amanda scratched her head. "He moved into your house. You adopted a pet dog together. He came to holidays. You went to Europe together."

"The dog was all his idea. No, sweetie, our relationship was more like companionship. But he's a good friend."

That wasn't true. Amanda knew better. Their relationship had been a curious mixture of compromise, jokes, and things left unsaid. Amanda hadn't always felt comfortable around the two of them, but she'd never been able to quite put her finger on it.

"Call it what you like," said Amanda.

Her mother dragged a finger along an axe. "I have friends to talk about this with," she said.

"I wasn't trying to—"

"Look at that," her mother said. She'd stopped in front of a large print of a black-and-white photograph. In it was the charred remains of what used to be a main street in a town. A small piece of cursive handwriting in the corner read *Lake Batonkin, September 5, 1913. Day after the great fire.*

Her mother stared at the photo for a while. "I don't remember what caused it. Do you?"

Amanda looked at the placard to the right. "Says here a careless innkeeper and his kerosene lamp. Six people died. Hundreds dove into the lake to escape the fire."

"Oh yes, now I remember."

"The structures were made of wood, so they must've burned up quickly."

"Terrible."

Mother and daughter stared at the print a moment longer. Then the old man at the front said, "Be sure you all see the schoolhouse out back."

"We will," said her mother.

The museum's backyard held more treasures. An old abandoned well that smelled of must and wet stone. A few faded garden gnomes with crabgrass tickling their feet, parked in the overgrown remnants of a vegetable garden that had been abandoned long ago.

There was a large anchor, taller than a person, and only God knew why it was there. Amanda ran her fingers along its smooth wooden flank. Nothing like that had ever been used in Lake Batonkin, and the nearest of the vast Great Lakes was at least sixty miles away.

"There's the schoolhouse," her mother said.

It was a clapboard structure, a classic one-room number from the nineteenth century. They walked over to the creaky door, and Amanda's mother tried to pull on it. It wouldn't open.

"Locked," she said. "I guess we'll just have to look through the windows."

The mother and daughter walked alongside the structure to the side windows. Amanda cupped her hands around her eyes and pressed her face to the dirty glass; her mother did the same.

"How charming," her mother said. "Look at the old-fashioned desks all connected front to back."

"And there's inkwells—" said Amanda.

"And dusty old books on the shelving in the corner—"

"And a little wooden stove in the middle of the room—"

"Imagine how cold it used to get in the winter—"

"It still does!"

Her mother stepped back. Then she gasped. "We have a visitor—look!"

Amanda looked over. Her mother was pointing at a deer, standing not more than fifteen steps away. The thing had one hoof up in the air as it studied them.

"I'm going to give it some food," her mom said.

"No," Amanda whispered, "don't do that."

"Why not?"

"It's not good to feed wildlife. They lose their fear of humans and sometimes their own family won't come near them either."

"I don't care, I'm going to—"

At that moment, the deer suddenly turned and bolted away. Three bounds, and it lifted itself up over the fence in a smooth huge leap. It landed on the other side and disappeared into the woods.

"I guess that ends that debate," her mother said.

Amanda felt the anger rising inside her chest. That old familiar feeling of being ignored and minimized by her mother. "Did you hear what I said?"

"Yes, of course."

"I don't think you did. I said you shouldn't feed wildlife. You said you don't care."

"So what?"

"So I'm a scientist. I work at the EPA. I'm preparing a report on zebra mussels."

"So?"

"So you have to listen to me."

Her mother made a show of opening her compact and fixing her lipstick. "About everything now? You know better than me?"

"About this, yeah."

Amanda stood there, her heart pounding, while her mother casually adjusted her makeup. "All right," she said simply.

"Okay," said Amanda.

"You can calm down now."

"I'm calm."

Her mother smiled sweetly. "Never let them see you upset, baby girl." Then she walked past Amanda.

Chapter Twenty-One

THEY DROVE BACK to the Sunset Cottages in silence.

Her mother smoked a cigarette, holding the little white cancer stick through the sliver of open air at the top of the barely cracked-open window. Next to her, Amanda mashed a bug against her window with her thumb. She looked at the bits of guts but made no attempt to clean it off.

That was her contribution to the day.

Her mother cleared her throat. "So what time do you want to get together tonight?"

"I'm really busy," said Amanda.

"Doing what?"

"Working. Like you."

"On the weekend?"

"I have nine interviews arranged starting on Monday and I'm still getting emails and calls."

"All right, so I'm on my own tonight," her mother said. "Fine."

Amanda felt bad. "Maybe I can call you if I get everything done."

"That's nice of you," her mother replied, her voice dripping with sarcasm.

Amanda silently rolled her eyes. "It's up here on the right."

They parked the car underneath next to Amanda's car, beneath a set of pine trees. Amanda's windshield and roof were covered in pine needles every morning, and tiny bits of sap had begun to collect on the finish. It was an old car, and she knew it wouldn't last much longer.

Her mother exited the vehicle and smoothed her shirt. "Do you mind if I come in?"

"Why?"

"I want to see how my daughter is living."

Amanda grew grumpy. "It's temporary, mom."

"I know. Let me see anyways."

"Why?"

"I'm your mother. I don't need a reason."

Amanda sighed, shrugged, and walked over to her cabin. Her eyes fell upon a piece of paper had been jammed into the door. That was curious. She pulled it out. It was a note.

Came by but you weren't here. Call me. 555-1432. -Tyler

Her eyes scanned the words as her mother came up behind her. "Secret admirer up at the lake?"

She hid the note. "Mom!"

"Who's the guy?"

Amanda's thumb had covered the name on the paper. "Just a guy. He works in town. We've been hanging out."

A hoarse shout caught their ears. "Miss Taylor! Well, knock me over with a feather duster!"

Lily had stumbled out of her cabin, glass tumbler of whiskey in hand. Her tank top was ripped across the midriff, and not in a fashionable way. Her unmanageable hair looked even more unmanaged than ever.

The property manager stumbled over, her leathery flat feet splatting across the packed sand, kicking small pinecones. Amanda's mother winced.

"She's harmless," Amanda whispered.

"But I remember her."

"Good golly," said Lily, "someone's been resurrected from the dead. Linda Taylor."

"It's Lisa," she said.

"Oh, I should've remembered that—your name is only a couple a letters off my own!" She guffawed. "I'm Lily, I don't know if you remember me."

"I do remember," said Amanda's mother.

They shook hands, Lily forcefully and Amanda's mother with hesitation.

"Your daughter doesn't know this, but I used to party with you and your husband sometimes."

"I wouldn't say that—"

"He was a good fisherman, I always liked his trout."

"I don't remember you coming over."

Lily shook her head and hocked up a loogie. It splatted on the ground near the wheel of Amanda's mother's car. "Whoa, that's a big one. Sorry you had to see that. No, your ex-husband used to go out on my ex-husband's boat."

Amanda's mother looked stunned. "I have no memory of that," she said.

"Shoot, my head's a block of Swiss cheese, and even I remember that," said Lily.

Amanda's mother gathered herself together. "I'm sorry, Lily, I've got to run." She turned to her daughter. "Baby girl, I hope to hear from you tonight."

"I don't know," Amanda admitted.

"Well then. Take care, Lily."

"Back atcha, hon," the woman said.

They watched Amanda's mother get back into her vehicle and pull away down the driveway.

"There she goes," said Lily. "I used to pester your momma so much."

Amanda turned towards her. "Why?"

"I dunno. I wasn't really in my right mind back then."

As opposed to now, thought Amanda. She was still smiling to herself as she entered her cabin and shut the door behind her.

Chapter Twenty-Two

THREE HOURS LATER, Amanda lay on her belly on her bed. The late summer sun was still hanging on, suffusing the room with a soft pink. It would stay that way until past nine o'clock.

In her hand was the piece of paper that she'd found stuffed in the doorway. Tyler had made time to come down to Sunset Cottages and check on her. The thought ignited a small, special feeling in her stomach.

A feeling she hadn't experienced in a very long time.

She'd just spent several hours emailing, calling, chatting, cajoling, coaxing, and fencing with members of the local public who thought they had tips about the local zebra mussel invasion. She'd become quite adept at figuring out who had something worthwhile. They usually spoke less. The ones who talked more usually had less to say.

Now she was officially done for the day. The phone number lay right there, scrawled in a bold, thick handwritten font that was somewhere between cursive and print.

She would call him.

Amanda dialed the number on her phone and put it on speaker.

"Hey," said Tyler's voice. He'd picked up on the first ring.

"It's Amanda."

"I know," he said. "What're you doing?"

She kicked a leg back and forth on the bed, a smile on her face. "Oh nothing. What about you?"

"I just put a six-pack in the fridge," he said. "You aren't going out tonight? The Spotted Pigeon has a darts tournament."

"No," she said. "I got your note. You want to come over? There's something I want to do."

"What's that?"

"Make S'mores."

He laughed loudly. Tyler seemed to like the thought of sticking a flaming hot marshmallow between two pieces of graham cracker and a slab of cheap chocolate.

"That is not something I've done in a long time," he said.

"Well, I'm going to make a bonfire, and you are welcome to join me," she said. Her heart was thumping in her chest.

"All right, let's do it," Tyler said. "I'll come over right now, before it gets dark. I'll stop at the store to pick up the stuff for S'mores."

"See you," she said. Then she hung up, maybe a bit too abruptly.

Inside, she squealed.

Twenty minutes later, Amanda had just carried the last of the chopped firewood to the fire pit on the beach when she heard the car roll up.

It was Tyler. He parked the vehicle and popped out. He was wearing a fresh red t-shirt and a pair of black jeans with gray flip-flops. A dark blue Detroit Tigers baseball cap was perched on his head.

"Hey," he said, "I brought everything we needed." He lifted up a plastic grocery bag dangling from his hand.

"Thank you," she said, "you're my hero. S'mores!" She took the bag and looked inside. She saw all the expected ingredients but there were also bananas and peanut butter and aluminum foil.

"What's all this other stuff?" she said.

"It's for something else. You'll see."

"All right," she said, skeptical. "But don't mess with my S'mores!"

"I won't! Can I put the beer in your fridge?"

"It's not really working," she admitted.

Tyler snapped his fingers. "Ah, I forgot. Well, Lake Batonkin it is."

Amanda giggled as he retrieved his six pack of beer from his car, went down to the water's edge, kicked off his flip-flops, and drove the cans down into the wet sand a couple feet past the water's edge. They were mostly submerged in the lakebed.

"They better not float away," she said, laughing.

"Wait, I've got a solution," he said, water up to his ankles. He scanned the water and then pointed. "Aha!"

Tyler went over a few paces and reached down into the water and hoisted up a rock about the size of a cantaloupe. Holding it on his shoulder, he carried it back over to the beers and placed the heavy weight gently on top of them, driving the cans down further.

"Now they won't," he said.

"Well done," Amanda said, clapping.

"There's something else to do," he said.

"What?"

He pointed at the stack of chopped wood. "We're missing kindling."

"Oh yeah," she said, "I did forget that."

Tyler cocked his head. "Let's head over to the woods, across the road. We can collect it PDF."

"Why did you bring up a pdf?"

"Pretty damn fast."

"Ah!"

Amanda walked with Tyler up the short driveway, across the road, and plunged into the woods on the other side of the street.

The forest was thick with gray pine trunks and was twice as dark as the beach had been. Thin whips of green pine needles dragged across her face and neck and shoulders, tickling. She realized that Tyler was no longer with her.

She turned and spotted him crouched nearby in a bed of low green undergrowth. He was picking up slender branches.

"Can I help?" she said.

"You can find some too," Tyler said.

But Amanda didn't move. She was staring at the greenery carpeting the forest floor around his feet. "Tyler, I think you're standing in poison ivy."

He stopped. Then he peered down to where she was pointing. The familiar three-leaved plant was all around him, brushing his feet.

"Oh crap."

He dropped the branches and leapt out of the area. "What should I do?"

Amanda said, "We go back to the cabin and see how bad it gets."

———

Ten minutes later, Tyler was sitting on the chair in Amanda's room, a grimace plastered onto his face. His bare feet were propped up on a towel spread across her bed.

"Oh God, it's starting to hurt," he said.

"I found it!" said Amanda from the bathroom.

She came out holding a small pink bottle. "Calamine lotion. It was here when I got here."

"Is it old?" he said, gasping.

She read the expiration date. "It expired two years ago. But shush, let's try it anyways. May I?"

He nodded, still grimacing. Amanda sat down the bed next to his feet and squeezed some of the lotion into her hands and began to apply it to his right foot. She tried to be clinical, but despite her best effort it slowly turned into a massage.

"That feels good," Tyler said, eyes closed. The grimace had disappeared from his face, replaced by a smile.

"Now give me the other one," she said.

He moved his other foot closer, and she repeated the process. While her hands worked the flesh on his feet, she tried to avoid looking up his legs, towards his thighs and beyond. Desperate, she searched for something to say.

"How's your mom?" she finally said.

"She's okay. Not doing the greatest health-wise, but, I mean, it's nothing too much to worry about."

"That's good."

The conversation paused. Then Tyler said, "How's yours?"

"My mom?"

"Yeah."

Amanda looked at him. "Funny you should ask that."

"Why?"

"She's here right now. In Lake Batonkin."

Tyler's eyes flew open. "No kidding. What's she doing?"

"She came to visit me, I guess. Just for the weekend." Suddenly Amanda felt herself seized by an idea. "What if I invited her to come over?"

"I guess so." He didn't seem thrilled by the idea.

"It would be so fun! We could all talk about the old days!"

"Sure," he said, "I'll be happy to see her. She was cool when we were kids."

"I have to warn you, she's got some personal problems—"

"Don't we all. It's family. It's a bonfire. Call her."

His eyes showed that Tyler meant business. Amanda went to the sink and washed her hands with hot water and soap. She knew that she was feeling uncomfortable being alone with Tyler. She knew that this was her way of coping with the situation. And she was fine with all that.

She called her mother.

"Hey mom? We're having a bonfire in a few minutes. Come over." She paused. "I did say we. You'll have to find out who it is."

Chapter Twenty-Three

AS THE SKY grew purple over the lake, Amanda kneeled in the sand next to the fire pit. She was setting up the pieces of wood like a log cabin. Two down in the sand, then two more crossways on top, then another two crossways on top of that.

"I think that's enough," she said, standing up.

Tyler sat on a folding chair nearby, his feet elevated on another folding chair. They were covered in calamine. "You need to go find kindling."

She whirled. "Don't tell me how to build a fire, Tyler Boyd," she said, eyes flashing.

Tyler lifted his hands. "Sorry. I wouldn't dream of telling you how to do anything." Then he muttered: "You still need to find more kindling though."

Amanda tapped a finger onto her lips. "Don't go anywhere. I have to find more kindling."

He saluted her with two fingers. "No chance of me leaving."

A moment later, an expensive sedan pulled down the driveway and parked. A woman stood up out of the car, wearing a pair of crisp khaki shorts and a sleeveless blouse. A pair of white earrings matched her white sneakers.

She looked around for a moment, then spotted Tyler. "Do you know who Amanda is?"

"You're her mother," Tyler said.

"I am," she replied, coming down onto the beach. "And who might you be?"

"I'm Tyler Boyd, ma'am," he said.

"Don't call me ma'am. It makes me feel old."

"Okay, Mrs. Taylor."

She grimaced. "That's even worse."

They shook hands. "I remember you when you were just a boy." Her eyes went to his feet. "What happened there?"

"So I went looking for wood in the forest and a patch of poison ivy leaped on top of me."

Amanda's mom winced. "Not much has changed since the last time we met. Where is my daughter?"

Tyler jerked a thumb over his shoulder. "In the same forest across the road. She's collecting the kindling that I dropped." He paused. "She's wearing shoes, don't worry. Have a seat?"

Amanda's mother sighed. "All right," she said.

She opened a folding chair and planted it in the sand nearby Tyler. Then she gently lowered herself into it and crossed her legs.

"It's a beautiful night," he said.

"So I'm probably not supposed to say this," Amanda's mother said, "but do you have a girlfriend?"

Tyler formed a ring with his lips and blew air out of his mouth. "Not at the moment."

"You like girls?"

"Yeah, I'm straight."

"I'm sorry—"

"No, it's fine—"

"It's just the mother in me," she said. "I can't help myself. Let's change the topic."

Twenty minutes later, Amanda was jamming the kindling horizontally through the slats of the small log cabin bonfire. It hadn't been lit yet.

"Maybe you should move that one," her mother said, pointing.

"Maybe you should let me do it myself," said Amanda.

"Never mind then."

Tyler watched Amanda work. "I want to help you so bad right now."

"We are prohibited," her mother said. "So Tyler, what are you doing with yourself?"

"My mom and I bought Hill's Drugs a few years ago. So we're running it now."

"Oh, that's nice." Amanda's mother chose her next words carefully. "I liked your mother. She was always pleasant."

"That she is," said Tyler. "Mrs. Taylor, can you pass me a beer?"

"Call me Lisa, please."

She pulled a bottle from the paper six-pack case and handed it to him. From his pocket, Tyler produced a bottle opener attached to his keychain. He popped open the bottle and slid the cap into his pocket in a single smooth move.

"Now the matches," said Amanda. She had prepared the log cabin well. "Here we go."

She struck a match and lit one of the pieces of newspaper that she'd placed next to the pit. Then she lit another, and a third. Soon a small fire was glowing. Amanda unfolded another chair and lowered herself into it.

"Well done," said Tyler.

"I'll take one of those, mom," said Amanda, pointing at the beer.

Her mother looked at her in mock indignation. "You are asking your own mother to beer you?"

"It's right next to you!"

She handed her daughter a bottle, a look of disapproval on her face. Tyler handed her the bottle opener.

Soon night fell, and a small white spot appeared in the sky. "Venus is out tonight," said Tyler.

"I thought that was a star," said Amanda's mother.

"Stars always twinkle. Venus is a solid little bit of white."

"You're still into astronomy," said Amanda.

"Yeah, a little," he said.

"How much is a little?" said her mother.

"I've been to a star-watching party."

"Ooh," said Amanda. "What's that like?"

He took a swig of the beer and listened to the fire crackle for a few seconds. "They do it in a field up in the hills. The real serious guys show up there for the weekend with RVs full of equipment. I brought my telescope but theirs are a lot better."

"So it's amateur astronomers," said Amanda.

"Mostly."

"Ladies, contain yourselves," cracked her mother.

"Mom!" she said. "Tyler just said he likes to go!"

Her mother crossed one leg over the other, and one arm over the other, and shrugged. "They're nerds, right?"

"I like nerds," Amanda said.

"I'm sorry," she answered. "You two, keep talking. I'll keep my mouth shut."

Amanda rolled her eyes but kept her mouth shut. Instead, she turned her attention to Lake Batonkin. The water was calm on this breezeless night, its waves kissing the shore gently and regularly.

A sound from the fire caught her attention. "What was that?"

"Tyler just threw something into it," said her mother.

Tyler was holding a banana-shaped piece of aluminum foil in his hand. "Here goes number two."

He shot it like a basketball into the log cabin, where it joined its friend.

"What are those?" said Amanda.

"It's an alternative to S'mores," he said. "They're called banana boats. You peel it open with one slit, scoop out some of the banana, replace it with marshmallows, chocolate, and peanut butter. Then you wrap it in foil and heat it up in the fire."

"That sounds delicious," said Amanda's mother. "You have three?"

"I do," he said, reaching into his bag. The third one bounced off the edge of the logs and ended up in the sand. "Could you fix that, Amanda?"

"Sure," she said.

She moved around the fire. The smoke from the wood was billowing directly into her eyes while she reached down for the aluminum banana and threw it into the fire. She wiped her eyes with the back of her arm, but she felt the tears coming down her cheeks anyways.

"There's been a lot of crying on this beach," said her mother.

That comment sent chills down everybody's backs.

"Yeah," said Tyler.

"Do you ever talk to Elsie's family?" asked her mother.

Tyler sighed. "I mean, I see her dad around sometimes. No, we don't talk."

"Why would you, I guess."

Amanda stood away from the fire with her hands thrust

into her pockets. Her eyes were burning hotter than the red embers. "Can we talk about something else?"

"Ignoring it won't make it go away," said her mother. "It happened. Elsie died. It's something that happened. Some children don't make it. Some of them drown."

She pointed with her chin towards the water out near the cape.

"Mom," said Amanda, forcing herself to keep her voice calm, "I am asking you to stop talking about this."

"Why?"

"Because I don't want to."

"You never want to talk about the hard things," she said.

Amanda erupted with anger. "You and dad never talked about the hard things! And you guys hated each other!"

"We just weren't right for one another, Amanda," she said.

"Nobody even knew why you were still together! My friends used to make fun of you!"

"Okay," said her mother, "okay, that's enough—"

"No," said Amanda, shaking her finger, "you brought this up! I asked you to change the subject, and then you criticized me for asking to change the subject! I'm sick of your criticisms!"

"All right," said her mother, standing up, "I know when I've overstayed my welcome. Tyler, you have a good night."

"You too, Mrs. Taylor."

Amanda watched her mother nod curtly at her. Keeping her head raised high, she turned and marched up the sand towards her car. A moment later, it started up and disappeared.

"She's so horrible," said Amanda, pacing the sand.

"You two are very different people," he said. Diplomacy at its finest.

"My mom has zero self-awareness."

"She loves you though. That's why she came up here."

"She hates it here. She hasn't even been to Lake Batonkin since she left my dad."

"Maybe we should change the topic." Tyler swigged from his beer, looking away.

A soft sound caught his attention. On the other side of the fire, Amanda was crying into her hands, back turned to him.

"Amanda," he said.

She shook her head. "I think I have to go to bed. I'm sorry."

"I'll be here if you change your mind," he said.

"Thank you," she said.

As she walked past him, Tyler put out his hand and caught her own. She turned towards him. "I'll check on you later. And if you ever want to talk, I'm here."

Amanda nodded, lips pressed tightly together. "Thank you."

He twisted around and watched her go up towards her cabin. He heard the door open, then shut behind her. Then it was silent again, except for the crackling of the orange fire and the lapping of the dark waves on the beach.

Tyler sat there, alone on the beach. He reached into his bag and produced a pair of tongs. Then he leaned forward and pulled the foil-wrapped banana boats out of the fire.

"Sure glad I made these," he said.

Chapter Twenty-Four

HER MOTHER CALLED at ten o'clock the next morning. Amanda was standing in the bathroom, wiping a soapy pad across her cheeks.

Seeing the name on the caller ID, she swore softly to herself. Then she picked up.

"Hi mom," she said.

"Hello darling," the voice said. She could hear background noise. "So I've decided to go home a bit early. I've got a very busy week and I'll need this afternoon and evening to prepare. I'm on the road right now."

"That's fine," said Amanda evenly.

"Are you sure?"

"I am."

"How much longer do you think you'll be at Lake Batonkin?"

"I don't know—until the project is done, I guess. Maybe longer."

"Couldn't you finish everything from Chicago?"

"No, I can't. Anyways, I like it here."

She heard her mother laugh once. It was a sharp sound, like a bullet flying out of its chamber.

"But Amanda, they're all so backwards up north. And you're not. You're educated. You're more sophisticated."

Amanda set down the pad and placed her hands on the counter and pressed. "Mom, I have more in common with some of these people than I do with people in Chicago. A lot of them are just, like, good people."

"If you say so," her mother sighed.

"I do say so."

"I also want to apologize for upsetting you last night. I did feel like I might've been interrupting something with you and Tyler."

"No, not really."

"He's quite taken with you. Maybe too much."

The conversation had now grown very uncomfortable. Amanda shifted her weight.

"What do you mean?"

"I mean that he's love bombing you."

"But he's not—"

"Honey, don't disagree. I've lived much longer than you have."

Amanda blew air out of her mouth and rolled her eyes upwards. "Fine. You're right. You're always right."

"Also, did you gain any weight? I thought you might've put on a few pounds."

Her mother waited all this time, until the morning she was leaving, to sink in that knife. Amanda looked at herself in the mirror, her stomach, hips, thighs, chest. She lifted her chin and looked at the flesh beneath. She raised an arm and checked for underarm flab. Nothing looked different. Everything was right where it'd always been.

"I think you were imagining that," she said.

"Maybe I was," her mother replied. "All right, don't be a stranger."

"Bye."

Amanda hung up without waiting for her mother's response. She dropped her face into her chest, took a deep breath, exhaled, and then lifted her face again.

"The people in Lake Batonkin aren't like her," she said aloud. "And I'm grateful for that."

Amanda stepped out of the cabin and peered at the beach. The fire pit was abandoned, nothing but a layer of blackened soot and creosote.

A small part of her hoped to see Tyler still sitting there: she hadn't heard him leave. She hoped he'd managed to get home okay with his blistered feet. She hadn't been in any state to think about him last night, that was for sure. Amanda had buried her head under her pillow for nearly a quarter hour, sobbing.

Her mother's words were sticking with her. Her comments about Elsie.

It happened. Elsie died. It's something that happened. Some children don't make it. Some of them drown.

That was true. Sometimes people die early, before their time. It's so simple that it doesn't even require stating. But emotionally accepting this fact is the real trick. It's harder to do than understanding the fact itself.

Amanda had always understood it, but she'd never really accepted it.

What would've happened that afternoon if she and Tyler had made a different decision?

Maybe Elsie would've lived.

She couldn't bear the thought and shoved it out of her

mind. Then Amanda crouched down on the sand, scooped a handful of sand, and let it run out between her fingers. She watched the grains silently disappear into the sand below.

A tear tracked down her cheek. She wiped it off on her shoulder, without touching her face. A bolt of emotional pain flashed through her midsection.

Then the moment passed. Amanda stood up, shook out her arms and legs. Then she turned away from the beach.

It was time to work.

As Amanda made her way out of the cottage later that morning, Lily's voice caught her ear.

"Hey darlin!"

Amanda turned. The landlord was leaning in her open doorway, smoking a cigarette.

"Yeah?"

"Just wanted to letcha know we're fixing the refrigerator and the stove tomorrow morning."

Amanda stood there, stunned. "You're kidding."

"For real. I got a couple guys comin' over."

"Thank you—it's been really hard without them."

Lily lifted her cigarette and pointed it at Amanda. "I got you. All taken care of, sweetheart."

"Sorry, but I have to run," said Amanda, getting into her car.

"Have a good one."

Chapter Twenty-Five

THAT AFTERNOON, Amanda stared at her knuckles on the steering wheel as she pulled up to her fifth and final destination.

She'd already met with four different local people, all of whom gave different explanations to her for the zebra mussels. Some were better than others. Evidently Amanda hadn't screened them well enough, because one elderly woman had clutched her arm and described in great detail why the mussels were actually planted by the government to destroy the whole region of Lake Batonkin. Amanda realized that the woman hadn't understood that the EPA was part of the government. She'd left quickly.

Another interviewee had told her interesting ideas about second- and third-order effects upon riverbank fishing. Amanda had made some notes on that one.

As of now, her total number of in-person meetings was just over twenty, and the number of phone calls to nearly forty.

The street came into view: Maple Avenue. Amanda turned

the car to the right and drove down the sleepy residential street.

This was the last chat of the day. The person she was heading to see, Gary Arnaudt, described himself as an amateur biology detective in his retirement.

She found the house. It was a cute two-story structure from the early twentieth century, painted forest green with orange shutters. It'd probably housed the town doctor or lawyer back in the nineteen-twenties. On the front lawn she saw an older man sitting on an outdoor wooden A-frame lawn swing. He wore a bucket cap and a vest with a lot of pockets down each flap. Large trees framed the scene.

It was idyllic.

Amanda parked the car on the street and stepped out. As she came up his short driveway, he stood up.

"Amanda Taylor?" he said.

"You must be Gary," she replied.

"That's right."

"Thanks for meeting me."

"My pleasure. Come inside."

Amanda followed the man. His stride was quick and energetic. They went up the steps onto the porch, where he'd already set out two glasses and a pitcher of water on a low table.

He pointed to two wicker chairs. "Have a seat there," he said.

Amanda sat down. He disappeared inside for a moment, then reappeared holding a notebook. He sat down on the chair opposite her.

"I don't know exactly what you're looking for, but I'll tell you exactly what I know. How's that?"

"Sounds like a deal," she replied. She clicked a pen and opened her own notebook.

"You're probably wondering about me. I'm a retired

lecturer at the community college down in Harrison. I was there for thirty-three years in the biology department."

Amanda wasn't surprised. He sounded a lot like every good teacher she'd ever had.

"Okay," she said.

"I saw your interview on WLBR news with Violet," he said.

"Yes, you said that on the phone."

He sipped from his glass, then studied it. "I care deeply about these waters, and this region, so I wanted to tell you something personally. Face to face."

The retired professor paused. Amanda felt her heart rate quicken.

"What is it?"

"There is nothing you can do to stop these new zebra mussels," he said.

"There's always something to be done—"

"Oh, there is something to be done," he said. "Of course. I can give you seven different things to be done." He tapped his notebook. Then he looked at her over his eyeglasses, as though she were a specimen. "But that's not going to stop them."

"What are you saying? That it's a losing battle?"

"Nature is much smarter than we are."

She sighed. "So I drove all the way out here just for you to depress me?"

"No," he said, laughing, "I do have some ideas for you to put in your report. But I was also curious about the type of young turk the EPA is sending out on these fact-finding missions these days." He studied her. "You look like one of the good ones."

Amanda blushed, then felt herself grow defensive. "Thank you. I feel like you have some opinions of the EPA."

"I do."

"Do you want to share them?"

Gary shrugged. "Your agency is sometimes helpful, sometimes damaging. It's very political. But mostly it's just irrelevant—in the big picture." He swept a hand around his head. "In the history of life."

"I like to think we're doing something useful. I mean, it's why I go to work."

"That's good," he said, leaning forward, pointing at her. "You'll need to remember that feeling as you get older." The professor sighed. "I've met lots of EPA folks over the years. It's sad what happens to most of them."

Amanda knew what he was referring to. She thought about many of the higher-ups at her office, and the burned-out expressions on their faces. They were cogs in a machine at the mercy of political elections. Long ago they'd realized that they couldn't help as much as they wanted to, and it cost them.

"Yes, well, I'm going to make sure it doesn't happen to me."

"You do that." He rapped his notebook. "Okay, let's start. If you're looking for a band-aid to cover your behind, I got one. Niclosamide."

Amanda ran through the files in her head. "I don't know what that is."

"It's an anthelmintic drug used to treat tapeworm infestations."

"That explains why."

"But beyond that, it's a general biocide. And there's some data suggesting that it could have an effect on the zebra mussels in narrow bodies of water such as creeks or small rivers."

"Oh good," said Amanda.

"Here," he said, handing her a document. "I laid it out for you."

She looked at the paperwork. Gary Arnaudt was generously handing her copies of his own research.

"But it only works in narrow bodies of water?" she said.

"To fill larger bodies of water such as Lake Batonkin, you would need a dangerous level of concentration. It's also expensive."

Amanda twitched her nose. This wasn't the silver bullet she was hoping for, but she could absolutely put this into her report.

Gary went on describing several other avenues of possibilities. Amanda took notes dutifully, asking questions.

Forty-five minutes later, Amanda finished writing and closed the notebook. "You've been a great help," she said.

"You seemed like you needed it."

"Is there anybody else you think I should talk to?"

He leaned back and tapped a finger on his teeth. "Sal Green. But good luck finding him."

That was the same guy that Curt Hooks had told her to find. "Someone else told me about him."

"Yeah, nobody ever knows what he's up to. But it's high-level."

"Let me know if there's anything I can ever do for you."

"There is something."

"What's that?"

Gary mustered a sad smile. "Take care of Lake Batonkin. In the future."

The way he said it nearly broke her heart.

"I will," she said.

She rose and shook his hand. As Amanda drove away from the house, she saw the retired professor waving at her from the porch.

Chapter Twenty-Six

THE NEXT MORNING, Amanda should've been thinking about the report. The final draft wasn't ready yet, and it was due on Wednesday morning. That was in two days.

But she wasn't. She was thinking about Tyler instead.

Something her mother said had stuck with her. *I mean that he's love bombing you.*

Amanda chewed on her lip. Hard to admit, but her mother might have been on to something there. Her mind raced through all the scenes from their relationship over the last month.

Tyler recognizing her in the store. Tyler asking for a mini golf and ice cream date. Tyler finding out that she was staying at Sunset Cottages. Tyler dropping in, unannounced, with pastries and childhood photos. Tyler leaving notes in her windshield.

My God. She could see it now. He *was* love bombing her.

Dazzling her with attention. Pushing for more time spent together. Bringing her gifts. Mirroring her own interests. Demanding that her mother join them.

She'd reciprocated every step of the way. God, she'd even

massaged calamine lotion into his feet. What was wrong with her?

Amanda didn't know why she hadn't been able to see it sooner.

She felt a sense of self-loathing. Why had she allowed him to continue to this extent? It wasn't like her. After all, she was an avoidant, just like her mother. She knew herself at least that much. She didn't let herself be carried away by anybody.

Not even Tyler. Her secret childhood love.

But that had stopped, abruptly.

Amanda made a fist with her fingers and squeezed hard. She would put an end to this, right now.

She looked at her phone. Tyler had called her twice yesterday. That felt ridiculous. Sunday was his day off. He should've been out doing other things, walking his dog, playing with his neighbor's kids, fishing, mud biking, or whatever else single guys did at Lake Batonkin on the weekend.

She swiped the missed calls off the screen and put down the phone.

At the library, she swept into the main room with the air of a woman on a mission. She nodded at the front desk and proceeded to her customary table and threw her backpack down onto it.

She felt a presence next to her. It was Dorothy, the friendly employee. Her hands were folded neatly in front of her once again.

"Amanda," she said.

"Yes?"

"We'd like to know if you'd be interested in using an empty office we have in the back. That would give you some privacy, and you can make phone calls there."

"That is *so* nice of you," said Amanda. "I would love that."

Dorothy led her behind the checkout desk, through a doorway. She found herself in a small corridor lined by six doors, three on each side.

The library employee led her to the last one on the right. "We used this room for storage until someone cleaned it out over the weekend."

"Was it you?"

Dorothy turned and winked at her. "I can't tell you that."

The room was bare: a simple desk with a simple chair and a very old office telephone. A narrow tall window admitted a vertical beam of yellow sunlight.

"This is lovely," said Amanda. "I really owe you."

"It's no problem at all."

"Is Karen here today?"

"No, she's off this morning."

"Thanks."

"Keep on doing the good things," the library employee replied. She smiled as she closed the door. Amanda sat down and opened her laptop and phone and got to work.

Her phone rang again less than an hour later. The screen read Stephen Grandulet.

Amanda was sweating. Getting phone calls from her boss was growing more stressful.

"Hi Stephen," she said.

"Amanda," his voice replied.

"I'm going to have the report by Wednesday."

"That's fine, but I need to see what you have tonight."

Panic shot through her body. "What? We agreed on Wednesday!"

"Yes, I know," he said. "But I've got a last-minute trip to

Minneapolis at the end of the week, so I won't have time to fix anything then. Let me do the fixes now."

"But I'm not done yet—"

He sighed. She could almost see him squeezing the bridge of his nose between his fingers.

"Tonight," he said evenly. "You will send me what you have tonight."

Amanda sighed. "Okay."

"And make sure you include at least one good solution, with evidence. It doesn't have to be perfect, but something. You're representing both of us."

"I'll do my best," she said.

"You'll do your best?"

"Yes. Bye!"

Amanda hung up the phone quickly. What was a "good" solution? Would the niclosamide research that Gary Arnaudt had given her be considered "good"? It only worked in narrow bodies of water. She didn't know.

There was a knock on the door. "Yes?"

Karen opened it, her pinched face already disapproving. "Hi Amanda, you can't work here, I'm sorry."

"But Dorothy—"

"Dorothy was wrong. You have to pack your things up and move back to the reading room."

Those two would never cooperate, but Amanda didn't have time to worry about them. As she closed her laptop, she felt the panic starting, for real.

Chapter Twenty-Seven

IN THE MAIN READING ROOM, Amanda worked on editing her report straight through the rest of the morning and part of the afternoon, pausing only to wipe sweat off her forehead and drink from her water bottle. She didn't even notice Karen's stares from behind the checkout desk.

At three o'clock pm, she closed her laptop once more and packed up her things and headed outside to the car. She stopped at a convenience store for a prepackaged sandwich and wolfed it down as she made the short drive out of town.

Back to Handley's.

The gravel pinged the underside of her car as the Trebuchet River zipped past on the right side. Soon she was pulling into the unfinished parking lot in front of the old store.

Inside, the fishy smell had abated somewhat from the other day. The sleeping spaniel was still sleeping. Behind the register, Harold Handley was studying a fishing catalog.

"Harold," Amanda said.

He looked up. Those forceful eyes found her and narrowed again.

"Amanda Taylor," he said.

That was funny. She hadn't remembered giving him her last name.

"You remember me," she replied.

"Indeed I do, indeed I do," he said. His hands hadn't lowered the catalog yet. He was waiting for her to give him a reason to do so.

"I have a few more questions about the zebra mussels," he said.

"I bet you do."

Harold's tone was different. He spat out the words nearly accusingly.

Amanda barreled on. "So I'm going to head out back to talk to the men one more time."

"No you aren't," he said. He set down the catalog at last, and pulled himself up to his full height, which wasn't much.

"Why not?"

"Miss Taylor, a few weeks back, you came out here telling us you were a student. Then we come to see on the news that you're actually an employee of the EPA."

Amanda lowered her head. That was correct. She'd lied to them because Curtis Hooks had cautioned her not to tell people that she worked for that agency. But then a few days later she'd gone on local television and blown that door wide open.

"Yes, that's true."

"You also told us you were a graduate student."

"That's true. I was a graduate student. But I finished the program."

"Recently?"

"Three years ago."

He shook his head. "Those men don't want to talk to you. They don't want to help the EPA and they most definitely don't want to help a liar."

Amanda sighed. She'd lied to stay out of trouble, but now that lie had gotten her into trouble instead. It was an impossible situation.

She looked out the window. Out on the floating docks, she could see the old leathery fishermen sitting on the white plastic chairs, brown beer bottles in their hands.

"All right," she said. "I'm sorry you feel that way."

"Have a good day now, and thanks for stopping by Lake Batonkin."

That was a dismissal if she'd ever heard one. Amanda began to leave the store. Then she stopped and turned back.

"Could I buy some smoked fish before I go?"

"How much would you like?"

"A pound."

"Trout or whitefish."

"Whitefish."

Harold went over to the refrigerated case and pulled out a chunk of smoked fish and plopped it on a piece of plastic wrap. He weighed it briefly. Then he wrapped it all in white butcher paper and stuck the printed-out price label onto it.

"Nine fifty-three."

She looked at him. "I'm trying to do good here, Harold."

He stayed impassive, no expression. "Nine fifty-three," he said again.

Amanda handed him a ten-dollar bill. He opened the cash register and gave her a pair of quarters.

"Have a good day," he said.

Amanda lifted the fish and made a circle in the air with her finger. "This is all in potential danger. I hope you understand that."

Then she walked out of the store. Harold's eyes followed her for a long time after she left.

Chapter Twenty-Eight

STEWING IN HER ANXIETY, Amanda pointed her car back towards town.

She was facing a serious problem. She had several half-measures to recommend for the zebra mussels, but none of them were really top-level. And that's what Stephen Grand-ulet was looking for.

Her career could be on the line. Not explicitly, but implic-itly. If this didn't go well, it could set up one of those situa-tions where she was quietly passed over for certain promotions. These little invisible slights would only become clear years later, when she was mired in mid-range office drone hell.

She needed a lifeline here. And the only lead she had left was the mysterious Sal Green.

But how to find him? She'd searched for him online, in the phone book, everywhere she could think. There seemed to be no record of this mysterious man. She wondered if she wasn't being led on an elaborate wild goose chase by the scientific community of Lake Batonkin.

Her phone rang again. The screen read *Tyler*. She didn't

want to talk to him right now, but she couldn't keep avoiding him. She muttered to herself and picked up.

"Yeah?"

His voice came through strong and clear. "Hey Amanda, just wanted to check in. Haven't heard from you."

"Most people just message, Tyler."

"I like phone calls. It's different."

"Phone calls are only for work," she said. "Everyone else just texts."

"Not me," he said. "I'm a man born out of time."

"I'm really busy right now. Like, I can't talk at all."

"You're talking at this second," he said.

"Look, I'm sorry about the other night," she said, changing the topic. The words came out fast and pressurized, like water from a fire hydrant. "My mom and I have a weird relationship."

"I remember."

"From when we were kids?"

"Oh yeah, your mom was always making snotty comments about the lake. She had a reputation here."

Amanda grew alarmed. That was news. She hadn't known that. But there was a lot about adult life that flies over your head when you're twelve years old.

"Then why did you agree to invite her the other night?" she asked.

"I thought it would be important for you to have your mother there. Family is important."

Amanda's eyes grew heavy and lidded. She was disassociating.

"Are you there?"

"Yeah, I'm here," she said.

"I want to see you this week, if you have time," he said.

There he went again, forcing a relationship.

"I don't know, it's just so..." She trailed off.

"It's just so what?"

"I need to get this done right now."

"Are you eating enough?"

"No, not really."

Something caught her eye. Up ahead, at the driveway to Sunset Cottages, a pair of firetrucks were parked. A local sheriff's deputy was there as well.

"I really have to go," she said, "something's happened—"

"What is it?"

"Bye, Tyler."

She disconnected and turned left into the Sunset Cottages.

Several firemen were conferring with one another around in the dirt driveway, beneath the overhanging tree branches. Nearby stood another man wearing jeans with kneepad pockets and a tool belt; he looked like he was on the verge of tears. Amanda had never seen any of these guys before.

Standing with them was Lily. She had her hands over her face and her eyes looked scared. When she saw Amanda's car, she threw her arms into the air and ran towards her.

Amanda slowed to a stop and rolled down her window. "What happened?"

Before Lily could answer, her eyes found the answer. The door to her own cabin was open.

There'd been a fire.

The structure wasn't burned down to the ground. It wasn't burned beyond recognition. But it was burned.

Lily was a blubbering mess. "I don't know what happened, I am so sorry hon, this is all my fault—"

Amanda parked the car and climbed out and stared at the disaster, mouth agape. Lily stood alongside her, explaining—

"The electrical guy finally came out to fix that outlet

behind the refrigerator and I don't know what happened, maybe he was trying to rewire something, but he said there was a shower of sparks and then everything just kinda went up—"

She made a *poof* gesture with her hands.

"What happened to my stuff?"

"I don't know, hon. It's real bad."

"Can I go inside?"

"No, sweetie, I don't think—"

One of the firefighters noticed Amanda starting towards the cabin. He came over and laid a hand on Amanda's arm. "I'm sorry, but you can't go inside until we secure it again."

"How long will that be?"

The firefighter shrugged. "We're waiting on another electrician to come. He's driving up from Kent County."

"Well, shit," said Amanda. She stamped a foot on the ground in despair.

"I don't know what to tell you," Lily said. "I can give you cabin five right over there but that one still needs some work done in the bathroom—"

"No," said Amanda, putting up a hand, "I don't want a different cabin. I want to live in a place with a functioning refrigerator, stove, and electricity."

"Yes, I hear that—"

"The EPA assigned me to your quote-unquote resort, I didn't choose it—"

Lily held up a pacifying pair of palms. "I get your frustration, it's been a rough ride for me these last few years, and I promise that you will end your stay very happy about that decision—"

"My stay is already ended," said Amanda. "I'm heading to a hotel. I only have two more nights anyways."

She stalked back to her car, and Lily chased after her. "Aw, come on now, let me make it up to you—"

"Goodbye, Lily," said Amanda.

She slid in behind the driver's seat, started the engine, rolled up the window, and put her sunglasses on. Then she backed around, put the car in drive, and left Sunset Cottages far behind.

Chapter Twenty-Nine

AMANDA IMMEDIATELY SPED THROUGH
DOWNTOWN. About half a mile beyond, on the lakeside
loop road, stood The Macarthur House.

It was the Victorian-era hotel where her mother had
stayed, full of lacy white architectural frills and pink-painted
siding. Amanda had no opinion about this place. Her mind
was laser focused on her report.

She parked in the lot next to a set of immaculately
trimmed hedges. Then she went up the short set of steps into
the lobby.

It was a bit like stepping into another world. She was
greeted by a riot of green, pink, and white floral décor. It was
papered on the walls, upholstered on the furniture, slathering
on the ceiling, embedded on the carpeting.

Amanda beelined for the front desk. A woman wearing
her hair in an updo looked up pleasantly at her. She was
wearing reading glasses and her face radiated wholesomeness.

"Good afternoon, are you checking in?"

"I'm not. I was wondering if you have a room for the next
two days."

"Oh dear," the woman said. Her face darkened. "That won't be possible."

"My mom stayed here last weekend. Does that help at all?"

"Oh! What was her name?"

"Lisa Taylor."

"I do remember her! A wonderful guest. You're her spitting image."

Amanda hadn't heard that in a long time. For most of her life, she'd heard people telling her that same thing. *Girl, you look just like your mother*. In the past, she'd grown accustomed to it, though today it hit different.

"Yeah, I know," she said.

"Were you already staying in town?" the woman said.

"I was staying over at Sunset Cottages but my cabin burned down this afternoon," she said.

"Oh!" the woman said. She jumped in her seat, startled. "You poor dear! Goodness! I wonder if I could've seen the fire from here."

She pointed out the large bay window. Off in the distance, on the beach on the other side of downtown, the tiny cabins of the Sunset Cottages were barely visible across the water.

"Maybe," said Amanda. "I wasn't there."

The staffer was looking at her face. "I recognize you. Aren't you that young lady who's here about the zebra mussels?"

"That's me," said Amanda. "I'm finishing up my report tomorrow and I need a place to stay."

"All right, let me make some phone calls and I'll see what I can find for you in town."

"That's nice of you," said Amanda.

"No problem at all. You can wait outside on the veranda and help yourself to a glass of ice water."

She pointed to a set of double doors. Amanda thanked her again and headed out through them.

The veranda was glorious, nearly as beautiful as anything in northern Italy or Switzerland. The long white balustrade, the green lawn, the game of bags—and the water. The blue surface of Lake Batonkin shimmered in the afternoon sun like a dream that had finally drawn within reach.

Amanda found the beverage station and poured herself a glass of water from a self-serve glass dispenser. Inside, yellow slices of lemon floated amongst the clear ice.

She dropped into a white-cushioned wicker chair and sipped the water. She felt her body still thrumming from the tension of the day.

The female staffer came outside onto the veranda. "I found you a place, Amanda. It's high season so this was the best I could do." She handed Amanda a note:

Day-Glo Inn, I-684 south of Braintree, $80.

That wasn't too far away. Amanda thanked the woman and left the hotel.

———

She set down her backpack in the musty hotel room and stared around.

The Day-Glo Inn was far from glowing.

The curtains were ratty, the carpet stained. The bedspread had seen better days sometime in the last century. She flicked on the light in the bathroom and found a few decades worth of damage, though it was clean.

Amanda seated herself at the cheap desk against the wall. The rolling chair was too low and the seat back was broken. But it would have to do. Sunset Cottages hadn't even had a desk, so this was at least an upgrade.

She opened her laptop and found the wifi network. She entered the code that the bored front desk clerk had written for her on a slip of paper. A moment later, she was on the network. It was slow but functioning, for now. You never knew with these cheap hotels.

It was time. Amanda sighed, put her hair up with a clip, and got back to work.

At seven o'clock, she emailed the latest draft of the report to Stephen. Then she walked down the road to a Coney Island hot dog stand on the roadside. It dated from the nineteen-fifties. Even though Amanda didn't care much for tubed meat covered in chili, she sat at a picnic table and wolfed one down. It wasn't enough, so she ordered another.

Next to her sat the owner's black Lab, whose orange eyes were fixed on her food. The eyes would move to her face, then back to the hot dog, then back to her face, then back to her hot dog.

"Beg all you want," Amanda said, "but you're not getting any of this."

Halfway through the second hot dog, her phone rang. It was Stephen Grandulet. She wiped her fingers off on the napkin and picked up.

"Talk to me," she said.

"It's not done yet," he said. "I like parts one, two, and three. But part four is lacking a novel solution. It can't be anything run of the mill."

She buried her face in her hands. "Yeah, I know," she muttered.

"What have you been doing up there? Laying on the beach? Drinking beer?"

"Stephen!" she said. "You know me. I've been working on this very hard."

Her boss backpedaled. "Okay, I'm sorry. I got carried away. Anyways, listen to me. I know I'm pushing you, but this is for your good and my good. I know what these people like to see, and you don't have it yet."

"Great, just great," she moaned.

"Do you have any more leads?" he asked. "Any more ideas? Any more people you haven't spoken with?"

Amanda stared at the grass at her feet beneath the picnic table. It looked green.

Green.

It made her think of Sal Green.

"There's one more person I haven't been able to locate yet," she said.

"Can you find this person tomorrow?"

"I'll try."

"Okay, keep me posted."

The call ended. Amanda suddenly had lost her appetite. Next to her, the dog was still waiting expectantly.

"It's your lucky day," she said, setting the rest of the hot dog on the grass in front of the animal. "Persistence pays off."

Walking back to the Day-Glo Inn on the shoulder of the road, Amanda was in a foul mood. Then her phone rang again. It was doing that a lot lately.

It was Tyler. Again.

She picked up, angry. "Look, I said I did not have time to talk to you—"

"I was thinking that maybe I could bring you something to eat—"

"No," she barked, "I don't want your food, I don't want to hang out with you, I don't want anything from you right now!"

"Calm down—"

"That doesn't help, Tyler. Did you know that? Telling a woman to calm down achieves the opposite."

"Maybe we'll just talk another time—"

"No," she said, switching the phone to her other ear, "I want to say something you need to hear. You have been love-bombing me."

"I've been lovebombing you?"

"Yes!" she said. A car roared past her, and she paused. Then: "All this showing me how great you are, how sensitive you are, how incredible you are, oh I was thinking about you. God, I feel like I'm being railroaded into a relationship! Do you see that?"

"I didn't know you felt this way," he said.

"I do! It's been bothering me for a few days."

"Then we'll stop talking for now. I won't try to communicate with you."

"Yes, thank you," she said.

"Fine," he replied.

"Fine," she answered.

A pause. Then: "Take care, Amanda."

He ended the call. Amanda walked up the driveway of the Day-Glo Inn and went up to her room.

She stood on the balcony looking out over the small parking lot. The red sunset was fading out over the dark tops of the trees. There was no lake, no beach here. Amanda's fingers tightened upon the railing.

Had she been unfair to him? Was she seeing it correctly? She didn't know. This was just how she felt.

Tomorrow would be another day.

She went inside her motel room and shut the door.

Chapter Thirty

AMANDA STARTED the day by driving back to Sunset Cottages. She had two goals in mind.

She pulled down the hard-packed dirt driveway and parked under the trees and then got out. She stood there looking at her former cabin.

The front door was closed and locked. A fresh pair of wooden boards had been nailed across it in the shape of an X. Through the window, Amanda could make out scorched and blackened walls inside.

She was here to pick up her stuff. She walked down to Lily's cabin and rapped forcefully on the door.

It opened. Lily appeared, bedraggled and confused. She looked nearly drugged.

"There she is," said Lily. Her eyes focused on Amanda. "Well I bet you came for your stuff."

"I did, Lily. And something else."

"It's over here. Hang on."

Lily disappeared, then reappeared in a moment dragging a clear plastic container along the floor. Inside were some of Amanda's items—a few clothes, a pair of shoes, her shampoo.

"Some of it was melted, like whatever that thing was you left on the bed."

Amanda looked through her things. She wasn't too torn up. She hadn't brought much of value, and she didn't value objects that much anyways. By her count, she was missing some clothes, one pair of shoes, and all her toiletries. It was nothing she couldn't recover.

Then she remembered something else.

The photos that Tyler had given her were missing. She covered her mouth with a hand.

"Oh no," she said.

"What's the matter, missy?"

"The photos. I had a plastic bag with photos in it."

Lily clutched her head. "I got everything I could, Amanda! Those firefighters were putting so much pressure on me to get out so they could board the place up, I just couldn't stand it!"

Amanda remained calm. "Can we get inside to see if you missed anything?"

"I didn't!"

"But you just said you only got what you could."

"Which was everything! I got everything of yours that I could, which was all of it!"

Amanda tapped her fingers against one another. She trying to stay calm.

"All right, Lily."

"Yeah, now let me take this out to your car for you."

She wouldn't hear any objections. The woman's spindly frame lifted up the heavy container and carried it out to Amanda's car, where they placed it in the trunk.

Amanda closed the trunk and turned to Lily. The cottage manager was sweating, but her eyes appeared a bit more focused than a minute earlier.

"You said there was something else?"

Amanda sighed. "Yes. There is."

"Well, go on. I'll make it happen. I swear it."

"You said you grew up with Sal Green."

"I did."

"I need to find him."

Lily blew air out of her mouth. "Well, that's a tall order. I mean, I can try, if you gimme a few days—"

"I need to find him today."

"Oh."

Amanda looked at her, expectantly. Lily's eyes darted around the horizon. "So I know there's places he likes to go, or at least he used to like to go. We ain't talked in some time now."

"You know where he lives?"

Lily shook her head. "Nope."

"What are these other sites?"

Lily crooked her head towards Amanda's car. "Get in and I'll show ya. You drive."

Four hours later, Amanda was leaning her head into her palm. She was in her car, parked in a space outside the local IGA. Her engine was running.

Lily was inside the store, hunting down an assistant manager whom she claimed knew Sal Green better than she did.

It'd been a chaotic day. They'd first stopped at the notary public to meet a man named Chuck who supposedly did a lot of paperwork for Sal Green back in the day. The woman working there told them that Chuck had died almost a decade earlier.

Next, Lily had dragged them to a bar that was connected to a hardware store. They were called Rick's Bar and Rick's Hardware, and they were two sides of the same structure, connected by a single door. According to Lily, the owner of both, who was unsurprisingly a man named Rick, knew Sal Green better than anybody.

They'd found Rick on the hardware side of the double business. He barely remembered Lily and then claimed to have no memory of Sal Green. He did tell them that he was having a happy hour special: one purchase of any overstocked tool earned you half off a pint of beer on the other side of the wall.

As they left, Amanda decided that either he or Lily was losing their marbles. Maybe both.

Lily had directed her towards a rectory, a locksmith, and a middle school. Each one had a different person who knew Sal.

None could recall very much about him. Amanda witnessed all the interactions and realized that she wasn't the only person in Lake Batonkin frustrated by Lily.

Now it was nearly two o'clock. She was miserable, resigned, despondent. Her professional life would be kneecapped by a mediocre report that she'd been handpicked to deliver.

Lily came back to the car and slipped in. "Welp, Matthew didn't come to work today. They said he's been having some issues with his cat. I started asking other people but nobody wanted to help me. I dunno why—I'm friendly, right?"

Amanda buried her face in her hands. This was painful.

"You okay, Mandy?"

"My name Amanda."

"Cheer up, things aren't that bad."

Amanda looked at the resort manager, stunned. "You let my cabin burn down, Lily. I can't finish this report the way he wants it. Things are *bad*."

The leather-skinned woman lit a cigarette. "Alright, you got a point there."

"I'm doomed."

"You got any other ideas?"

Amanda thought hard. "I mean, the only thing Curt Hooks told me was that Sal liked to hang out at the duck park."

"Then let's go to the duck park. You got nothing to lose."

"Why don't I know the duck park?"

"You'll see. Head west on Ossineke Road."

Her spirits lower than they'd ever been, Amanda put the car into gear and wheeled around and left the grocery store.

Chapter Thirty-One

AMANDA AND LILY stood at one end of the covered bridge that crossed from the mainland to the island.

The island was, in fact, the duck park.

About fifteen miles west of Lake Batonkin was a low-lying area filled with a complex welter of slow-moving rivers, streams, and islands. It was easy to forget that it wasn't a stagnant lake, but was in fact a shallow piece of interconnected Midwestern quasi-swamp.

Amanda had never been here before. She looked around, in a small amount of awe. "This is beautiful," she said.

"I bet those zebra mussels are havin' a ball here," said Lily.

"Probably," said Amanda.

Lily gestured towards the parking lot, which was filled with nine other cars, even in the middle of the afternoon on a weekday. "There's folks here, so let's cross over and find out who."

They crossed the covered bridge and found the trail that looped around the small island. Amanda walked ahead, hands in pockets, enjoying the riparian climate. She'd grown up in this part of the country, and it was filling something in her soul.

"Hey there's some kids," said Lily. A pair of boys were kicking a small soccer ball down the woodchip path.

"Sam isn't a kid," Amanda said.

"True," Lily said. "He's five years younger than me."

"I thought you were in the same class together."

"We were," said Lily. "I wasn't the best student."

Amanda chewed that one over for a while.

They followed the woodchip path, past the oaks, the maples, the elms. A classic rope hung from a tree branch over the water, waiting for a group of kids to find it. They passed a set of teenage girls, a pair of elderly men.

"You see him?" said Amanda.

"Nope."

They rounded a curve and found an etched wooden map of the island mounted on a pole. They studied it.

"Let's go there," said Lily, pointing to a small bay. "I bet he could be over there."

"This is ridiculous," Amanda muttered.

"Hey this was your idea," said Lily.

"Come on."

———

Twenty minutes later, they turned off the main loop and plunged into a very narrow path through the pine forest. Small tendrils of plants whipped Amanda's face and hands.

"Why did you choose this bay?" she said.

"Oh, cause Sal always liked frogs and I figure that this little bay probably has 'em."

They moved through the forest, the sun dappling their shoulders through the trees above. The thick scent of natural growth filled Amanda's nostrils. Part of her wanted to stay lost in these woods forever.

With no warning, they arrived at a tiny wooden dock at the edge of the water. A pair of little boys were standing there, cheap fishing rods in their hands. A canoe was pulled up onto the narrow little strip of dirt shore.

"Hi," said Amanda.

"Hi," said one back.

"Catch anything yet?" said Lily.

The boys shook their heads no. Amanda looked around. The water here was brown with sediment and growth. Gentle swirls decorated the surface of the water. A family of ducks swam past.

It was peaceful.

"Look at that," said Lily. She was pointing out at a small open boat, a couple hundred meters away. A lone figure with black hair sat in it.

"Do you think that's him?" said Amanda.

"I can't tell," she said.

One of the boys silently held out a pair of binoculars. Lily took them and lifted them to her face.

"That looks like Sal," she said. She passed them to Amanda, who studied the distant figure hunched over in his boat.

"He's always loved floating around alone," said Lily. "Like I said, he don't want people to find him."

"We have to talk to him," Amanda replied.

Lily clapped one of the boys on the shoulder. "Hey, you mind if we steal your canoe for a few minutes?"

The boys looked cautiously at one another. They shrugged. "It's okay," said one.

"You're such good boys! We'll bring it back, promise. And if I don't, you can throw eggs at Sunset Cottages."

She barked a laugh at the boys. They looked confused.

Amanda crouched down and said, "We'll be just a few minutes, I promise. We wouldn't abandon you here."

"Okay," one said.

Lily had already launched the canoe partway into the water. Amanda climbed in, and the canoe rocked wildly. She kept her arms out for balance, then sat down on the front seat and picked up a paddle. Lily hopped in the back and picked up the other. They both began paddling.

It was easy pushing across the water and they made it towards the small boat quickly. As they drew closer, Amanda saw the man wasn't fishing. He was hunched over, and appeared to be writing.

"Sal Green, is that you?" shouted Lily. "Long time no see!"

The man looked up. Amanda felt a thrill.

"Hello?" the man said.

"It's Lily!"

"Oh—hi Lily."

"I got somebody here who wants to talk to you."

Chapter Thirty-Two

SAL GREEN WAS a fiftyish man with a full shock of black hair. His face was jowly and his thick lips hung open as though in perpetual surprise. On his torso was a worn-out black t-shirt with small holes around the collar. It should've been consigned to a pile of rags.

"I'm Amanda," she said.

"Yeah," said Sal. He wasn't looking at them.

"How you been, Sal?" said Lily.

"I've been fine," he said. His voice had an odd sing-song affectation.

"We were looking for you all day," said Amanda.

"Sorry you couldn't find me," he said. He was staring off at the horizon.

Amanda noticed a notebook on his lap. "What are you doing there?"

"I made some measurements and now I'm tabulating them and tonight I will be reorganizing them into structures that will be useful to the problem I'm trying to solve."

"What's the problem?"

"Do you know about the zebra mussel?"

Amanda tried to contain her delight. "I do. They're an invasive species."

"They are a danger to this ecosystem and somebody needs to stop them. But it's going to be very hard to stop them so I'm focusing on the best way to limit or at least control them."

He was a literal thinker, that much was for certain. "I work with zebra mussels too," she said.

"Oh really?" he said, brightening up.

"I do. Can you show me your work if I show you mine?"

"Okay," he said. He sat up straight in his boat and held the notebook out across the water. "See, here is the pH concentration for all my samples, and after that—"

Amanda stopped him. "Why don't we all go to shore and you can show me there?"

"That sounds good," he replied. "Better, actually. We can go over there where I like to park my boat."

He pointed to at a small dock adjacent to the parking lot.

"Thanks Sal!" said Lily. "See ya shortly!"

"Okay," he said.

The two women paddled back towards the boys. "Can I ask you something?" said Amanda.

"You can try," came Lily's reply, "and maybe if you get an answer, we'll both be surprised."

"Do you think Sal is on the autistic spectrum?" said Amanda.

"Well, I don't know anything about that," replied Lily. "We just always knew he was odd."

"He'd better be there."

"You got nothing to worry about," said Lily. "Sal don't want to be caught—but once you do catch him, you can't get rid of him."

Twenty minutes later, they reconvened on the grassy bank along the water, facing the duck park island.

Amanda sat next to Sal, reading through his notebook. He had a plastic bag of white grocery store bread. He was blithely ripping the slices into small pieces and feeding the ducks that had surrounded them.

"Sal, what's this mean?"

He glanced at the page. "It's four different invasion models. I broke it out by strength of vector."

Amanda studied the work. It was astoundingly good, at least from her point of view. She closed the notebook. "Sal, what do you do for a living?"

"You mean my job?"

"Yes, what is your job?"

"I was a chemical engineer at Dow."

Amanda's eyebrows lifted. "That must've been a lot of work."

"Yeah, I guess. But they didn't want me anymore."

"Why?"

"I don't know."

"You don't know?"

"No." He shredded more bread and threw it on the grass. The ducks drew closer, muttering small quacks.

"Did you leave, or did they fire you?"

"I left. But they made me go."

"Why?"

"I saw some things that they didn't want me to see."

Amanda said nothing. She thought it wiser not to ask questions about the darker side of chemical companies.

"So now you're an independent researcher."

"Yes, but only in the subjects that cross over with chemistry. It makes sense to research those things because in those areas I have the greatest chance of success."

Amanda nodded. "I understand. Have you published anything?"

Sal shook his head. "The journals don't think independent researchers are serious." He looked at her. "What do you do, Amanda?"

"I work at the EPA. I'm putting together a report on the zebra mussels."

"Oh wow."

"What do you think is the best solution to the problem?"

He thought for a moment. "I think it's biocontrol through genetic modification technology."

She nodded. That had been an area of research that she had neglected so far. There were only so many hours in a day.

"What specifically?" she asked.

"It's not about the new tools. It's about the strategic deployment of them."

She held up a finger. "But it's about the tools too. You cited some CLPM-image analysis system. Do you know that the dual change score model is being adapted from the social sciences for use in this sector?"

Sal stopped ripping the bread. He looked at her with respect in his eyes. "You know a lot too."

"Not enough. Is it okay if I use your research?"

Her heart pounded in her chest as she waited for his response. He thought about it.

"Yeah, that's okay."

She quietly clutched the air with a fist. "Thank you, Sal! You're a prince. Can I take the notebook tonight?"

Growing nervous, he reached out and took it back. "I don't let anybody have my notebook."

Amanda's mind raced. "Okay, how about this—if you come with me to my hotel room tonight, you can read while I use on your notebook."

He looked horrified. "Your hotel room?"

"Nothing sexual is going to happen," she reassured him. "It's just the best place to work."

"Okay," he said, relieved, "I guess that's fine."

She exhaled. "Terrific. Thank you! But we have to go, right now."

"What about Lily? Is she coming too?"

Amanda stood up and looked around. She spotted the property manager, dead asleep in the car.

"I think she's ready to go."

Chapter Thirty-Three

AT ELEVEN O'CLOCK THAT NIGHT, Amanda sat back in her squeaky chair and dropped her hands by her sides.

"I think that's it," she said.

Behind her, Sal Green lay on his belly on her hotel bed. He was looking through a vintage comic book from the nineteen-seventies.

"Do you have any more questions?" he said.

"I don't. You explained everything beautifully. This is really good work."

"It takes a lot of good work to get results."

"Yeah, there aren't any shortcuts." Amanda pulled out her phone. "We don't have a photocopier, so I'm going to take photos of these pages for my records."

"Okay."

She arranged the notebook under the desk lamp to get the best possible light. Then she snapped photos.

"Tell me about you," she said.

"Okay."

She waited. Then she realized that he wasn't going to offer any information. "Do you live with anybody?" she asked.

"I lived with my mom until she died three years ago."

"So now you live alone?"

"Yeah."

"Do you have anybody special in your life?"

"No."

"No friends?"

"Sometimes people call me and try to talk to me but I don't know what to say."

"Lily said you used to play with frogs."

"I don't remember Lily."

"She was my friend that was with me today. You went to school with her."

"Oh."

Amanda raised an eyebrow. This was why nobody could find the elusive Sal Green. He had trouble even comprehending what basic relationships were.

She finished snapping the photos. "Sal, I'm going to take you home now, and then I'm going to put the finishing touches on this report."

"Okay," he said.

Driving him back to his house, Amanda looked over at the man. Sal was the closest thing one could be to a treasure: hard to find, but full of wealth once you claimed it.

At five-thirty in the morning, Amanda finally finished her report.

"Wow," she said aloud.

It ran thirty-four pages and nearly eight thousand words. It was dense with research and footnotes. This was exactly what her graduate training had prepared her for. Not many people could say that.

She hit save, then saved again as a pdf file. Then she opened her browser.

Connection failed.

Ugh. Amanda reset the network connection and tried again.

Connection failed.

She tried a few more times, even restarted her computer, but no luck. The hotel Wi-Fi had been patchy all day yesterday, and now it was down for good. If she'd been more tech-savvy she could've set up a hot spot, but Amanda hadn't ever bothered to learn how to do that.

She'd have to go into town to find Wi-Fi. And with almost everything still closed so early in the morning, she knew where she'd be forced to go.

The famous golden arches welcomed her like a pair of arms.

Amanda strode into the dining area of the McDonald's with an exhausted scowl on her face. She'd just pulled an all-nighter and now here she was in the belly of the damned.

She approached the counter. The cashier looked as tired as she was. "Welcome to McDonald's how may I help you?"

"Egg and cheese McMuffin."

"Anything else?"

"A tall coffee."

"That'll be seven eighty-nine."

Amanda paid and collected her food and went to a plastic booth. There, she opened her laptop, logged into the McDonalds Wi-Fi, and opened her email. She composed an email to Stephen, explained that the report was finished, then attached both the Word and the pdf files.

Then she hit send.

She sat there staring at the screen for a minute. It was over.

She took some of the egg sandwich in her mouth and began chewing. She felt a wave of exhaustion wash over her. She put her head down on the table.

———

"Hey, Amanda," a voice was saying, "wake up. Come on now, wake up."

She felt a hand shaking her arm. Amanda opened her eyes. She was still in McDonalds. The dining room was busier now.

Standing over her was a young woman covered in doodle tattoos. It took Amanda a minute recognize her.

"Rachel?" she said.

The woman's two little kids were wrestling each other nearby. "I thought you said you wouldn't be caught dead in McDonalds?"

Amanda thought about it. "I was trying to die. You interrupted me."

Startled, Rachel took a step backwards. Amanda put her head down and went back to sleep.

Chapter Thirty-Four

FIVE O'CLOCK THAT AFTERNOON, Amanda burst out of the waters of Lake Batonkin like an exultant trout.

The water was clear and cool and blue, and the droplets shone on her face as she stood there, breathing, in chest-deep water. She'd just returned from swimming across the bay.

All these weeks up here, and she hadn't found time to enjoy the thing that made her most happy—until now.

She looked towards shore. She was at the public beach in downtown Lake Batonkin. Families, children, teens—everyone was out today. Sandcastles and brightly-colored beach toys dotted the strand left and right. The pier stood out to her left like an image from a vibrant painting.

Amanda emerged from the water and breathed out. It felt good to swim here. It felt good to be here.

Life just felt good.

Her report was good too, evidently. Stephen had called her that afternoon, waking her up in her hotel bed. "This is exactly what we need," he'd said. "Let's talk tomorrow night, I have to run. Oh, and take the rest of the week off before you come back to Chicago."

Before you come back to Chicago.

Those words didn't sound as attractive as she thought they might've. Amanda had mumbled something in response, then hung up and dropped her head back onto the pillow.

Now she walked out of the water, up onto the beach. She was wearing her cutest yellow bikini, the only one that got her the occasional compliment.

She stood there, soaking in the sun, not knowing where to go, or what to do, and not caring either.

Amanda Taylor was alive.

"Am I allowed to say hello?" said a man's voice.

She turned to the right. Tyler was coming towards her, wearing a tight t-shirt and a pair of camouflage shorts. He'd gotten a haircut, was barefoot, and his dog walked ahead of him in his bouncy little shuffle.

"Tyler, are you stalking me?" Amanda said.

"You're stalking me," he responded. "You know I walk my dog here at five o'clock every day."

"That's not why I came here," she said.

"I'm going to need proof of that."

"I can't give you proof of my intentions."

"Well then," Tyler said, "what can you give me, Miss Taylor? Anything?"

She dandled one foot behind the other. She guessed it looked cute in a bikini. "An apology?"

"For what."

"Being short with you. Saying things I didn't really mean."

He nodded but didn't say anything. He looked like he was thinking about something else.

"Will you come with me?"

"To where?"

"I'll show you when we get there. Are you busy?"

"No."

"Get some flip-flops on."

Amanda crooked her head, curious. "All right."

A few minutes later, she found herself standing at the open gate to the Calvary Cemetery.

"This is where you wanted to take me?" she said.

Tyler didn't respond.

"Will you say something?"

"No," he said. "You told me I was being too overbearing and dragging you into a relationship. So this is me not saying anything."

"Why are you taking me here?"

He took Amanda by the hand and pulled her into the cemetery. She knew where he was taking her.

"I haven't visited since the funeral," said Amanda.

"She's right over there," he replied.

A moment later, they were standing in front of a headstone. It read *Elsie Armstrong*, along with the dates that she'd lived.

"Twelve years old," said Amanda. She felt a tear coming up. "Just think what she could've been. And if we hadn't said no that day—"

"We don't know that's true—"

"But in my heart, I feel like it's true—"

Tyler grew upset. "Listen, she was going swimming across the bay with or without us. You know that, right?"

"I mean, I guess—"

"And then she didn't make it."

"But she *asked* us—"

"And?"

"And we said no because—"

"Because why, Amanda? Why didn't we swim with her that day? Let's talk about it."

She spun around, looking at the cemetery. "Because we were here."

"Doing what?"

She couldn't meet his eyes, though she knew that they were boring holes into her own. She'd spent years trying to drown this memory.

"What were we doing here, Amanda?"

The words came out like soft pellets. "We were kissing each other, Tyler."

Amanda's first kiss, here in this cemetery. Age twelve.

With Tyler.

They'd sought refuge behind a large family memorial monument. They'd spent the afternoon sitting cross-legged on the cool grass beneath the oaks, holding hands. Nobody'd been there. They'd been alone, in their own private world.

She'd kissed his lips again and again. He'd run his fingers over her face.

All while Elsie drowned.

Normally the three of them would have swum together. But on that day, they'd decided to leave Elsie and find a place to make out. They'd planned it.

And when Elsie had asked them to go swimming, Amanda still remembered the glance that she and Tyler had given one another.

I can't, I'm going into town with my mom, she'd said.

I've got baseball practice, Tyler'd said.

It'd been the last time they ever saw her.

The weeks afterwards had been a blur of tears, guilt, and confessions.

She and Tyler had only seen each other twice more that summer. The first time was a contentious meeting of all three children's families, which ended in a screaming match between Elsie's mother and Tyler's father.

The second was at Elsie's funeral.

That was the last time she'd been at Lake Batonkin.

She and Tyler quickly fell out of touch, and Amanda hadn't ever shaken off the feeling of guilt. In the years that followed, she'd unconsciously associated the act of kissing with the deaths of her friends. Deep down, Amanda knew that this tragedy had affected her relationships.

"We have to put this behind us," said Tyler.

He was holding her by the arms and staring into her eyes.

"I know," she mumbled.

"It's affected me," he said. "I can't fully commit to a relationship. I come on strong, then I back off. It's been the same, ever since."

Amanda wiped her eyes with her shirt. "Yeah, me too."

"We need to do it again. Can we? Let's try one more time —and make it right."

Amanda felt his fingers lift her chin upwards. She opened her eyes. His face was inches from her own.

"Amanda Taylor," he said.

"What?"

"Kiss me."

Before she could respond, their lips met.

Plotworks Publishing

If you enjoyed this story, please leave a review at the place where you purchased it.

Then visit Plotworks Publishing to find other stories to enjoy!

Now turn the page for a sneak peek at another *Finding Home* novel!

GIRL
seeking
FARM

*a finding home
novel*

It's been
waiting for her
all this time.

HANNAH DOVE

Girl Seeking Farm

Jessica stepped to the curb at the small airport, dragging a pair of heavy duffle bags and a fabric suitcase. She smelled the air.

It smelled rich and humid. Like home.

A white Ford F150 was approaching her. It was spattered with mud around the bottom edges and sported mud flaps behind the rear wheels. Jessica cocked her head. She hadn't seen a vehicle like this in a long time.

It pulled to a stop. The driver's door opened, and a tall, gangly man stepped out. He was wearing a simple plaid shirt, jeans, and a pair of well-worn work boots. His face was broad and his high cheekbones looked sharp enough to open cans. His face said trustworthy.

"Young Billy," she said. "It is *so good* to see you."

"Likewise, kiddo." Young Billy wrapped his long arms around her and gave her a long squeeze. It felt better and lasted longer than any hug she had ever received in the city. "Nonna is real excited to see you. That's all she's talked about for the last two weeks."

He bent down, lifted her bags, and easily tossed them into the bed of the truck.

"There is some breakable stuff in there," she said.

"Sorry, darling," said Young Billy. "The pigs aren't quite as sensitive."

She climbed into the passenger seat of the cab. It was clean. In the dashboard was a satellite radio.

Young Billy eased the car out of the pickup zone and onto the freeway. When they'd left the airport far behind, he finally exhaled. "Congestion makes me get all worked up. I need my elbow room. Coffee?"

He gestured to the cup holder, where a paper cup was waiting.

"For me?"

"Of course. I brewed it this morning."

Jessica smelled it. "Drip coffee?"

"Oh. Let me guess. You probably like espresso now."

Young Billy was right—there had been a mandatory cappuccino break every morning at *Spretza*—but Jessica decided it was better not to admit that. She replaced the paper cup back in the holder. "I'm okay for now."

Young Billy reached forward to the satellite radio. "It's goin' to be a long drive, and I'm not much for talkin', so we'd better put some music on."

He hit the power button, and the sounds of lap-steel guitar exploded out of the speakers. He immediately turned it down. "Sorry. I like it kinda loud when I'm by myself."

She listened to the music for a while. In perfectly clear enunciation, the singer was complaining that he couldn't ever get drunk enough to forget his problems. Jessica hadn't heard any music like this in a long time. In New York City, she'd only listened to Dutch electronic beats, which were challenging. This music, though, was neither. It was exactly what you expected, exactly what you wanted.

"What do you think?" said Young Billy.

"Of what?"

"The music."

"It's not my favorite."

"This is Blake Shelton. He's my favorite. He's got a really good voice."

She shrugged. "It's okay, I guess."

"Stay out here for a while, and you'll come to like it."

The truck rolled off the highway, turned west, and headed out into the rolling fields. Jessica's stomach rose and fell as the vehicle floated up and down the gentle crests and troughs.

Young Billy rolled down the windows. "Let's get some fresh air in here. You probably haven't smelled this in a while."

Jessica inhaled deeply. The smell of clover, of pine, of earth filled her nostrils. It was alluring.

"That smells great," she said.

"You can't get tired of it," said Young Billy. "So, there's something I should probably tell you about."

"What's that?"

"There've been some changes at the farm recently. We sold the Holsteins."

She nodded. "Nonna told me last year."

"No more dairy. The new regulations were impossible. We just got out completely. It's easier this way."

For a moment, Jessica lost herself in nostalgia. During her two years on the farm, she'd been assigned the job of milking the family's three dairy cows. It'd been strange at first, squatting on the stool, squeezing the teats, but she'd quickly grown used to it. Of course there'd been plenty of modern equipment that could have done the task, but with only three cows, Nonna had said it was unnecessary. Mostly, she hadn't wanted to invest in the machinery, not when your granddaughter would do it for free. In New York, Jessica had noticed that people tended to stare, then burst into laughter, when she admitted to knowing how to milk a cow, so eventually she'd stopped talking about it.

Soon the land flattened out, and Jessica felt a stab in her heart as she recognized the local general store.

Hackmore's.

It'd been done up like a big red barn, even though it was a normal concrete structure underneath. She was glad to see that it had stayed the same. The big sliding front doors were still in place. The bales of hay out front. It still even had the adorably hick sign, a man in overalls with a hayseed in his teeth.

"Good to see some things don't change," she said.

"That's not exactly true," said Young Billy. "Hackmore's goin' through some rough times. The old man died last year, and his kid doesn't want to keep it open."

"Why?"

"The corporate farms don't buy so much as a single seed there. They got their own distributor for everything." He shook his head. "Hackmore's is antiquated. It's from another time."

"I remember playing on the sacks inside when I was little."

Young Billy smiled. "I played on those sacks too. Don't get me wrong, we buy from them when we can, because I'd hate to see them close. Jesus, I'd have to drive sixty-five extra miles, one way, just to get a few extra bags of feed."

A few miles later, the plains were broken by a stand of trees that ran parallel with the road. Alongside the trees, about thirty meters in, was a creek.

Jessica craned her head. "The creek hasn't changed either. Still tiny."

"When those thunderstorms roll through," he said, "you better stay the hell away from that creek."

"I remember," she said.

He suddenly grew serious. "No, it's *worse* than you remember."

"What do you mean?"

"I don't know why the weather has changed, but everything's real screwy now. Every year for the last six years, that creek floods higher and more often than before. Last year it ruined Kilkenny's soy crop."

Jessica remembered how Kilkenny's property was at least a hundred meters away from the creek. "That's pretty scary," she said.

He nodded. "You'd better believe it. Personally, though, I think it would take an act of God for flood waters to touch Nonna's toes. And if they tried, she'd probably point her finger and tell that dirty water to jump right back to wherever it came from."

Jessica laughed. Feared but respected, her grandmother was not a personality to be taken lightly.

As Young Billy slowed the truck, Jessica felt her heartbeat speed up. There, on the right, was the familiar long deer fence —actually two fences, about a foot apart, to discourage jumping.

Then the driveway appeared. The simple sign hadn't changed: *Nonna's Farms.*

Jessica felt the warmth spread like syrup through her body, first in her thighs, then up into her chest and down into her feet. If there was any place on earth that needed to stay the same, this was it. And Nonna was making sure of that.

Young Billy cranked the wheel of the truck, and they rumbled down the dirt road, the bare springtime fields on either side, towards a distant structure.

Nonna's house.

Plotworks Publishing

Turn the page for another sneak peek into a Hannah Dove cozy mystery! If you enjoy pet bunnies, baking, and murder, this story is for you—

BOOK 1

a cozy mystery

MURDER BUNNY

and the

Carrot Cake Caper

A baker has been murdered. His pet rabbit is on the case. Let's hop to it!

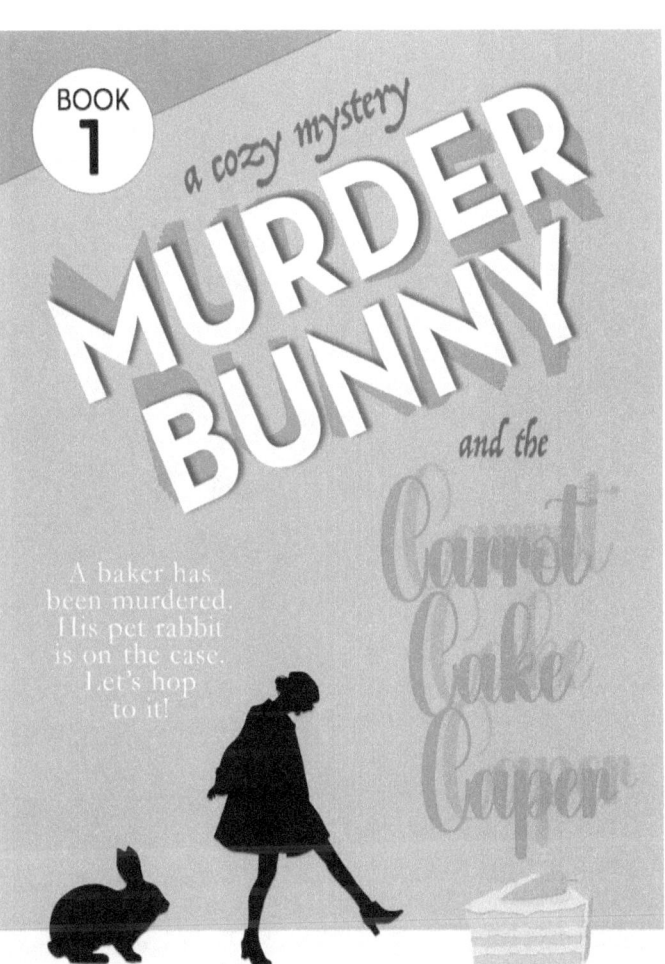

HANNAH DOVE

Murder Bunny and the Carrot Cake Caper

Goodness gracious, this day has been horrific. Yet it started out so positively that I can't quite make heads or tails of it.

I saw Nigel, my now-dead owner, wake up this morning feeling very enthusiastic about the qualifier round of the baking competition.

I watched him closely, as is my habit. He paced around the kitchen in his lavender terry cloth bathrobe, a mud mask on his face, going on and on about how he was certain to sail through the qualifier, about how the world wasn't ready for his newest recipe. He was right. Nobody was ready for that recipe. Nigel had come up with the greatest carrot cake that I'd ever nibbled.

And that's saying a lot, since I'm a bunny.

Anyways, Nigel carried on and on about cream cheese frosting, commitment to one's art, and how the most precious commodity in this world was enthusiasm. Nigel was always rambling on like that. He loved to address me, asking questions and then answering them. As usual I said nothing. I've found it's better to play stupid in the company of humans.

Everybody wants a dumb bunny.

Anyways, he was all a bit too much for me. As the rant continued, I hunched down in the corner of my hutch, nibbling on my morning watercress and scented lemon water, listening. The one good thing I will say about Nigel is that he always kept me stocked in the very best food and beverage.

I shall miss that about him.

At noon he emerged from his bedroom fully dressed in his white baker's outfit. I ran circles around the hutch for a few seconds, pretending to be excited. We have to embarrass ourselves, us bunnies, to keep a roof over our heads.

"Fluffy, if you continue behaving yourself, someday I'll let you inside my bedroom." He crouched down and peered at me. I could see the cream glistening on his mustache. "But until then, it's not for animals–no matter how cute." His finger jabbed at me through the squares of the cage, and my nose twitched involuntarily. I hate it when that happens.

It's both funny and sad that Nigel assumed I'd never seen his bedroom. Even given his posh British accent, with his plummy vowels and endless wit, he never figured out that I could open my cage. He never noticed the bits of pine shavings that I inevitably tracked out when I went out for my late-night adventures in his home. Maybe he'd mistaken me for a silly Pomeranian. That's fine.

Again, everybody wants a dumb bunny. So that's what I give them.

Nigel removed his recipe book from the cupboard and lay it gingerly upon the table. The recipe book had a combination lock on it, if you can believe that. He only opened it when nobody was around, and kept it locked and shelved at all other times.

Of course, I'd sussed out the four-digit combination long ago. You never know when you might need to know something like that.

I watched him lay the book out on the countertop and dial the combination and open it up.

"And so it begins," he announced to nobody. I watched him begin to assemble the ingredients. Flour, sugar, butter, eggs, carrots, vanilla essence. A series of unmarked containers with mysterious ingredients that his pudgy fingers handled with reverence. It was all a mystery to me.

But I had faith in Nigel. He'd worked for months on this carrot cake recipe, and he had the track record to prove it.

Next, he pulled the black cover from his red KitchenAid mixer and ran a loving finger along its edge. Nigel guarded the machine like a national treasure and spent his evenings cleaning it.

I curled up in my wood shavings and started to read the paper. You humans assume I can't read because I'm a bunny, but what you don't realize is that I've spent most of my life living on top of newspapers. They line the bottom of my cage, beneath the pine shavings, and I've learned about everything that you can learn from a newspaper, from news to sports to politics to lifestyle to weather to advertisements.

Nigel started the mixing, using both hand and machine. "See, Fluffy, what they don't know is that the texture starts at the beginning. It's the combination of the two." Later, he lovingly poured the batter into three different cake pans and massaged them with his silicone spatula. He slid the pans into the preheated oven and paced the kitchen while it baked, the sweet aroma of ginger and carrot floating through the air.

When the kitchen timer rang, Nigel sprang towards the oven. He removed the cakes, let them cool for exactly six minutes on the counter. Then he began assembling the finished product, handling the disks with great care, gently smoothing the cream cheese frosting between the layers, and finally coating the entire cake.

When it was finished, he removed a small box from a

cupboard. He opened it and gingerly removed a small bell tower, only a few inches high. "See this, Fluffy?" Nigel said. "It came into my store almost a year ago. It is the *perfect* topper. This is going to win me a sixth title."

He gently placed the bell tower on top of the cake. Then he backed away, rubbed his hands together, and giggled.

"I am the best," he said.

I twitched a skeptical whisker.

"What? It's not bragging if it's true."

Half an hour later, the cake was boxed up and in Nigel's car. He had put on his trenchcoat and begun humming to himself. I didn't know his intention, but I wasn't going to let him leave without me. I'd traveled with him to the fair each of the last five years. I'd suffered the fingers of pink frosting thrust into my hutch, the bits of oatmeal cookie that children dropped onto my back from above.

Spending a week at the county fair wasn't my cup of tea, but I refused to be left alone. He didn't know it, but Nigel needed me.

Drawing in my breath, I stood up on my hind legs, gripped my cage with my paws, and rattled it using every ounce of my strength.

Nigel stopped in the doorway and turned. "What's that, Fluffy? You want to come?"

Fluffy. The name made me nauseated. I never liked that diminutive. Still, I began leaping, just to make my intentions clear.

"Well, that's a surprise." He stroked his chin. "I thought that you didn't enjoy the fair last year."

I shook the cage harder, then did a cute flip.

Nigel sighed. "All right, I suppose you could come this year." He picked up my crate by the handle and carried me outside.

I was quite fond of Nigel. He usually did what I wanted.

———

At the fair, Nigel got a couple of the local kids to set up the tent in exchange for some biscuits he'd made. He wasn't going to waste his carrot cake on them. Wise. Children have no appreciation for good food. Sticky little creatures think anything with enough sugar is delicious.

Nigel rested my hutch down in the corner of the tent and began setting up his cake station in the center. Today was all about flavor, but Nigel was a showman. He'd brought a stand and the belltower and even a set of tiny lights. He loved a good presentation and said that it was the reason for his win.

One by one, people trickled over while he was preparing his cake. I recognized a few of them. They'd be competing with Nigel in the contest. A lot of them offered him some of their own foods to try. I could tell from the look of triumph on his face and the condescending compliments that none of their desserts could approach the magnificence of Nigel's carrot cake.

As they chatted, I lay in my hutch, watching their feet and waiting for the cooing to begin. Sure enough, it did. *Oh my look at him.* Then: *What a beautiful little creature!* Finally: *Be careful or he might end up on my plate!* I twitched my whiskers and pretended to giggle at that one. You have no idea how many times I've been sweetly threatened to end up on somebody's plate.

The crowd died down. The occasional person would come in and speak with Nigel, but I paid it little attention. There was a lump of frosting stuck on my ear. No amount of scratching with my paw seemed to be getting it off. It was driving me crazy and keeping me quite preoccupied.

That's when I heard a thump, and then a cry.

Nigel had fallen over, onto the ground. I couldn't see his face but something was definitely wrong. I don't know if he was breathing or not.

I wondered if I ought to break out of my cage and go for help, but I saw another pair of feet. There was another human in the tent. I assumed they would sound an alarm or call for help of some kind, whatever it was humans did when someone suddenly fell to the floor clutching their chest.

The feet vanished, and I waited. Surely, someone would come soon.

It was a few minutes before another pair of feet appeared. I heard a girl calling Nigel's name. She screamed.

The next hour was a flurry of activity. I saw legs, calves, and feet, but I couldn't see Nigel through the crowd. I heard the anxious voices conferring closely. By the time the paramedics arrived, I began running in frantic circles in my cage, but nobody noticed me. Dumb bunnies get forgotten. I watched them put Nigel on a stretcher and wheel him away.

Then a pair of black police shoes arrived next to my cage. "We'll have to take this bunny to a shelter of some kind," said a male voice. "It doesn't seem like Nigel has anyone in the area to take him."

"A shelter?" said another voice. "Could as well just let him free, y'know? The shelter's only going to end up putting him down."

My ears went flat. I felt the panic rising in my haunches. Did I get a say between those two options? Because I definitely chose freedom. I began to run in circles trying to communicate this choice. I didn't know what else to do. Sometimes it worked, sometimes it didn't.

They weren't looking at me.

"Don't say that," the first man said. "He'll be fine. The animal shelter's not that bad."

Then my cage was lifted up. I saw the humans. They didn't stare at me like I was used to, however. They were too busy examining the tent. I looked around and spotted Nigel's display table. The lighting, the decorations, and the cake stand were all there.

However, the carrot cake that Nigel had spent the morning obsessing over had vanished.

The officer kept carrying my crate, taking me out of the tent. I didn't have time to dwell on the missing cake.

I could feel my heart thumping. This was very bad. I had to deal with one problem at a time. I couldn't survive in an animal shelter. They'd toss me in a little crate with a bunch of other rabbits. They'd feed me pellets. I'd have to tolerate the dumb bunnies' dumb conversation. It would be torture.

In the midst of my panic, I gazed out at the crowd of humans around Nigel's tent. That was when I saw her.

A young woman wearing a conservative yellow gingham print dress. It had a ruff around the neck. Her dark hair was cut in a conservative bob and her fingers were interlaced around a small clutch. Her eyes were large and sensitive and even a little watery. She looked like someone who needed a bunny.

And she was looking at me.

I had to act fast. I flipped my body around and kicked open the cage door. I knew exactly how to make it look like an accident. Then I leaped out onto the ground and hopped straight over to the woman. I sat on her shoe and leaned my head against her shin and began trembling.

"Oh my goodness," she said.

"He likes you, Agnes," said the police officer. He came over and looked down at me. I was really shivering now. It wasn't easy to look this vulnerable but I knew that my future depended upon it.

"I'm unsure about what to do."

"Agnes, would you be willing to take care of Nigel's bunny for a while?" he said.

She looked down at me. I looked up at her. Our eyes met.

"Yes, I suppose I will," she replied.

Plotworks Publishing

Now turn the page to discover the world of Castor's Grove!
Orphan's Egg is a sweet paranormal romance by A.J.
Renwick—

CASTOR'S GROVE

ORPHAN'S EGG

a young adult
paranormal
romance

A.J. RENWICK

Orphan's Egg

Frances West stood, frozen on the sidewalk, staring at the familiar gray door.

It was the first thing she'd recognized since returning to Castor's Grove three weeks ago. Though she'd been born in the city, Fran's time in it had felt less like a homecoming than she'd secretly hoped. The streets were easy to navigate with buildings organized in square grids, her temporary apartment on the edge of downtown was clean and conveniently located, and there was nothing lacking in the environment. With the ocean on its south and east borders, forest to the north and west, and dense urban high-rises in its center, Castor's Grove was a city that boasted something for everyone.

But there was nothing special about a city that everyone could enjoy. Fran liked it, but it was in the same way any visitor might. While waiting to hear back from the adoption agency, she'd wandered the streets, avoiding the usual tourist activities, waiting to see something that sparked some long-buried memory or wander into someone who would recognize her.

Now, it was happening.

But instead of the sense of belonging she'd imagined, Fran's chest tightened, and her breath caught. Her anxiety buzzed in her brain.

There was an image of a sword burned into the door. It stretched almost the entire length of the door, its hilt hovering only a few inches above a sunflower welcome mat that looked far too normal in the context. Who lived in this house?

Your foster parents. Fran grappled with her anxiety to take control of her own thoughts. *They're probably into Dungeons and Dragons, or one of the kids they cared for did it.*

Either way, it was nothing to worry about.

Fran took a deep breath and pushed her hands into the pocket of her large black jacket. It wasn't cold, but she wrapped it around her as she walked up the steps. There was no doorbell. She tapped her elbow against the wood.

No response came from within. Fran could've tried again. It had been a light knock.

This is too weird. They might not even live here anymore. What was I thinking just knocking on their door?

She should just leave a message. There was paper in her pocket; she could buy a pen somewhere nearby, write a letter, and slip it into the mailbox.

"Upon my honor."

Fran spun around to see a thin middle-aged woman with olive skin. Short gray hairs frizzed around her temples, narrowly escaping the band that pulled the rest into a black ponytail. She wore an oversized green dress with a canary yellow jacket that matched the shopping bag in her hand.

The woman took a few steps closer, keeping her eyes on Fran. There was a wariness to her expression.

"Um, I was just—"

There was nothing suspicious about knocking on someone's door in broad daylight, but Fran felt suddenly guilty. "Do you know if the Franklins still live here?"

"We do." She narrowed her eyes, glancing between Fran and the door as though she thought the teenager was blocking her path. "Is this a university project? Are you doing a census?"

Fran was tempted to lie, tell Mrs. Franklin yes, and bolt, but she'd made it this far, so she shook her head. "No, I'm not with the university. I'm actually, well I was, one of the kids you fostered. It was like fifteen years ago. You probably don't remember—"

"Frances Buckler."

The sound of her original name rang like a bell in Fran's ears. Her lips mouthed the word *Buckler*, trying to wrap themselves around the harsh first syllable and the slur of the second. She'd whispered it to herself every night since she'd learned it, but it still felt like it belonged to someone else.

"It's Frances West now, actually."

"You've dyed your hair." Mrs. Franklin reached toward her, and Fran flinched away, but she was too slow to stop the woman from grabbing a clump of black hair. She ran a finger along it as though testing if the dye would rub off. Then she dropped the hair, pulled a set of keys out from her bag, and turned to the door. "Come inside. You shouldn't be out here."

"Oh." Fran pulled her jacket tight again. Her first instinct was to refuse. Stranger danger and all that. But how did she expect to get information about her parents if she didn't talk to Mrs. Franklin? "Maybe for a minute, but I can't stay long."

The strange yet familiar door led to a normal and therefore relatively forgettable living area. There was a fireplace in the corner with olive green couches and a squat brown coffee table. Paintings of flowers hung on the walls.

Fran's stomach tightened as she stepped in. *Why doesn't it match the door?*

"Sit." Mrs. Franklin instructed, pointing at the couch.

Fran hesitated, but the woman kept smiling and staring.

Eventually, she gave in and sat on the edge of one of the chairs. Mrs. Franklin didn't join her.

"You must tell me about your life, dear. What's brought you back to the city?"

"Nothing in particular," Fran said, fingers crumpling stray pieces of paper in her pockets as she tried to guess what Mrs. Franklin's angle was.

There's no angle. She's just a nice older lady who took care of me for six months when I was a toddler. Don't listen to your anxiety.

"Although, I was wondering if you knew anything about my parents," Fran forced the truth out. "I wouldn't bother you about it, but there's no record of them anywhere, no birth certificate on file for me, but you're the one who recorded my last name as Buckler, and my dads said you sent that gift with me, so I just thought, maybe you'd known them?"

Fran held her breath as she waited for Mrs. Franklin's response. This was it. Her former foster parents were her last chance of learning the truth about her birth parents. Who had they been? What had they done? Had they loved her?

The woman before her might have those answers.

Mrs. Franklin's smile faltered. "What gift?"

"You know," Fran said. If the woman had been able to recognize Frances after fifteen years, she must have remembered it. "The Fabergé egg. It's purple with gold details."

Mrs. Franklin's smile stretched so tight that it looked like her skin would snap. "You still have that?"

"Obviously." Sarcasm leaked into Fran's voice before she could stop it. Did the woman really think she'd have thrown away the only gift she'd ever received from her parents?

"It's here with you? In the city?"

Fran stiffened, feeling her heart thump in her chest. That was a strange question. It wasn't just her paranoia.

"No. I left it back in Lansing."

"Excuse me a moment. I need to make a call." Mrs. Franklin spoke with the smile frozen on her face.

Fran nodded. Her eyes flicked to the front door. It was close, but not so close that the older woman couldn't grab her before she got to it.

Mrs. Franklin didn't leave the room. Eyes trained on Frances, she pulled a phone from her pocket, pressed a button, and raised it to her ear.

Fran struggled to keep her breathing steady as she stared at the woman.

"Dammit." Mrs. Franklin's smile finally dropped as she lowered the phone. She knelt on the carpeted floor before Fran and rested her hands on the teenager's knees.

Fran was small, but the woman before her was frail. She could push her off. But her body was frozen. All she could think about was the fact that she should've hidden her knife in her pocket instead of her boot.

"Listen, Frances, I have the answers you want, okay? But we need to be honest with one another. What's the address of your home in Lansing?"

There was no way Fran was telling her that.

"Never mind. Two dads, West? I'll look it up. Just wait here until I'm back, okay? I'll tell you about your parents then."

Before Fran could fully process what the woman had said, Mrs. Franklin had raced out of her own house. The tension in Fran's body slackened as she realized that she was alone, but her heart continued to quiver. This was all far too weird, and try as she might, Fran couldn't pierce through her anxiety to come up with a logical reason for Mrs. Franklin's actions.

I need to leave.

But Mrs. Franklin knew her parents. Fran could finally learn who they were, who she was.

The longing burned within her, begged her to stay, just as

her anxiety screamed at her to run. The result was that Fran sat on the olive chair for a lot longer than most sane people would have. And she might have remained there until Mrs. Franklin returned were it not for the noise.

A loud twang shook the floor beneath Fran's chair.

That settled it. She leaped up and grabbed the door handle without hesitation. But it wouldn't budge. Mrs. Franklin had locked her in.

Crap.

Trustworthy people didn't lock teenagers in their houses. Whatever claims Mrs. Franklin made about her parents could easily be false. She couldn't stick around.

But how could she escape?

The Franklins' house had only one entry, and there were bars on all their windows. Except for the ones in the basement.

It was the design of all the houses in this area. Fran had noticed it while walking through the neighborhood. But the strange noise had come from the basement.

Fran reached into her boot and pulled out her knife. Fingers trembling, she managed to get the blade free. She held it before her, afraid to breathe as she searched for the basement door.

It didn't take her long to find it in the kitchen.

Cold sweat trickled down Fran's back as she stared down a long flight of steps. There was no sound now save Fran's own pounding heart.

Maybe the noise she'd heard was a cat. People owned those. They knocked things over. At least, they did in television shows.

And I think I'm too smart to die in a horror movie? This is the dumbest thing I've ever done.

But waiting for Mrs. Franklin would've been just as foolish. So Fran tiptoed down the stairs, knuckles white around her knife.

A stream of light from a high window illuminated the bottom of the staircase. The tension eased from Fran's body. It was too high for her to climb through, but there might be a ladder or something she could stand on down below. Maybe she wasn't about to die.

"Dust!" a boy's voice exclaimed.

Or maybe she was.

"Couldn't you at least give me a few minutes to try to escape? Maybe we could make a trade?"

Fran's legs turned into metal rods, anchored to the ground, unable to move. Her heart did its best to escape them. It took all her effort to turn her head toward the voice.

Her mouth dropped open. The only thing that stopped her from gasping was that her chest was too tight to let the breath escape.

Trapped underneath a silver net was a boy about her own age with a mass of red curls. But it wasn't the net or the color of his hair that made Fran feel as though she were about to faint.

He had wings.

Plotworks Publishing

Be sure to visit our store at Plotworks Publishing to discover even more titles to enjoy!